Comin

Home to Collingsworth
Book 6

by

Kimberly Rae Jordan

THREE**STRAND**
P R E S S

A CORD OF THREE STRANDS IS NOT EASILY BROKEN.

A man, a woman & their God.
Three Strand Press publishes Christian Romance stories
that intertwine love, faith and family.
Always clean. Always heartwarming. Always uplifting.

∽ Chapter One ∾

THE wailing of a siren jerked Nate Proctor from deep sleep. He rubbed his eyes and stared up at the ceiling for a moment. Where was he? It didn't take long for the sleep to leave his brain. A motel. In Sanford. He'd decided to stay there after spending the day in the town instead of heading home.

When the sound of the sirens didn't fade, he looked toward the window. Red light intermittently flashed across the thin curtains. It too did not fade. He glanced at the LED display of the clock that sat on the nightstand beside the lumpy mattress he lay on.

2:13

When another siren joined the first, Nate stumbled from the bed and across the room to the window. He pushed aside the curtain and looked down the street. Shock held him in place for about two seconds before he scrambled to find the jeans he'd been wearing before bed. As fast as he could, he jerked them on and then pushed his arms into the sleeves of his shirt. Skipping socks altogether, he jammed his feet into his shoes and, after grabbing his phone, he headed for the door of the dingy motel room.

He sprinted down the sidewalk, did a quick check for traffic then bolted across the road toward where the fire engines were stopped, their lights still sweeping against the night sky. When a wall of heat slammed into him, Nate skidded to a stop.

Surely this was a bad dream.

It had to be.

"Sir, you need to move back!" The full-suited firefighter reinforced his statement by placing a gloved hand on Nate's chest and pressing.

Move back?

Red hot flames flickered and roared as they slowly, but determinedly, consumed half his livelihood. Nate took one step back to appease the man, but he refused to move any further away. The firefighter moved on to other people standing nearby.

When nothing remained between him and the blazing building, the heat once again hit Nate. The hair on his arms stood on end and his skin felt singed—even blistered—by the fierce heat. Flames continued to dance and burn, lighting up the summer night sky as the fire spread across the roof of the building.

Waves of heat battered his body as he stood, hands on his hips, watching the flames reach high into the dark sky. When the smell of burning rubber and oil assaulted his senses, Nate blinked rapidly to keep his eyes from watering. As much as the heat burnt his skin, his insides were chilled.

This was arson.

And he had a pretty good idea who was responsible. But right now he was trying to accept the reality that once the flames had wreaked their havoc, his auto repair shop would be nothing but a blackened, charred structure.

The crowd grew as people stumbled from their beds to see what the commotion was about, but Nate stood alone watching as firefighters worked to put out the flames.

"Are you the owner?"

Nate glanced away from the fire to see a tall man in firefighter gear standing next to him. He gave him a quick nod and looked back at the garage.

"Not going to be much left," the man said. "We're doing our best, but given the nature of the business and the products you kept on site, the fire spread rapidly."

The man was right, but Nate knew he ran a safe workplace. He followed all safety requirements and protocols. It was something he emphasized with the staff at both of his garages, the one here in Sanford and the one in Collingsworth. The fire should never have gotten this out of control unless the sprinklers had been tampered with prior to it being started.

"Are you up for some questions?" the man asked.

When Nate nodded, the man gestured to a nearby fire truck. "Let's get back a little from the heat. It's not safe for you."

As reluctant as he was to leave his business, Nate needed to let someone know about his suspicions. The noise of the fire lessened a bit as they moved away, enough for him to hear his phone ring.

Frowning, Nate pulled it from his pocket where he'd shoved it on his way out the door earlier and stared at the display. *Dean Marconett.* A knot formed in the pit of his stomach. A call from the sheriff at this time of night couldn't mean anything good.

Had something happened to Lily?

Please, God, don't let it be Lily.

"Hello?"

"Nate? You're okay?"

Nate rubbed his forehead. *Okay* might be a stretch. "Basically. What's up, Sheriff?"

"Where are you?"

"I'm in Sanford. Currently watching my business burn to the ground."

There was such a long pause Nate wondered if the call had been disconnected but then the sheriff said, "Well, we have a situation on our hands here in Collingsworth, too. Your house was set on fire earlier."

Nate was sure he hadn't heard the sheriff correctly. "My house?"

"I'm so sorry, Nate. It started about an hour ago and was fully engulfed by the time the fire engines got there. We thought you were inside." The sheriff let out an audible sigh. "I can't tell you how relieved I am that you're okay."

His house? The only home he'd ever known? The place that held most of his happiest memories? The pain that sliced through him threatened to take him to his knees. He had to push that aside to deal with later. Now was not the time.

He swallowed hard, willing away the emotion that wanted to flood him. "What about the garage?"

"Looks like there was an attempt to start a fire there, but it never really got going. Just one corner of it was really damaged. Kinda looks like the person setting it got spooked."

"So you believe it's arson?"

"Oh, without a doubt. All signs are pointing in that direction. And you said the business there in Sanford was hit as well?"

"Yes. I'm watching it burn right now. Doesn't look like there's going to be much left of it." Nate was surprised he was able to speak so normally. The chill that had invaded his body earlier was giving way to numbness as he absorbed the news the sheriff had given him

"I suppose you'll need to deal with things there tomorrow, but give me a call as soon as you're back in Collingsworth."

"I will." After he said goodbye, Nate lowered the phone to his side, clutching it tightly in his hand. How much more was he supposed to take? Three devastating hits to his life in three years. Lily. His dad. And now this. There wasn't much left that could be taken from him at this point.

Nate felt a touch on his arm.

"You okay, son?"

Nate glanced over. He'd forgotten about the man standing next to him. "Sorry. I just got news that my home in Collingsworth was also set on fire, and an attempt was made on my garage there."

"Really?" The large man looked toward the fire. "Guess we're going to find some proof of arson here, too, then. Three fires on one person's property seem a little too much to be accidental."

"You might want to call the sheriff there in Collingsworth. Dean Marconett. He was the one who called me and could give you details of what happened there as well."

"I'm sorry about this," the man said as he clapped Nate on the shoulder. "I've heard good things about your business. Word was you ran an honest, affordable place."

"I tried." Nate gazed again at the inferno in front of him. "Guess it doesn't matter much now."

"Do you have any idea who might have done this?"

"Nate!"

Hearing the shout, Nate swung around to see the man he'd hired to be manager of the Sanford garage jogging in his direction.

Marty Stevens came to a stop next to Nate, his gaze on the garage. "I couldn't believe it when Drake called to tell me what was going on."

Nate knew Marty's younger brother was part of the fire department in Sanford. No doubt he'd recognized the address when it had been called in. "I got a call from

Collingsworth. They set my house on fire and made an attempt on my garage there, too."

Marty draped an arm around his shoulders and gave him a quick hug. "I'm so sorry, man. It's Chip, isn't it."

"Chip?" This time it was the man to Nate's right who spoke. "You think you know who did this?"

Before Nate could answer, Marty said, "Yes. We had to fire Chip Lassiter last week. He was not a happy camper."

"Why did you have to let him go?"

Again Marty spoke first. "He was doing shoddy work and then overcharging for his time. We also suspected he was telling customers that parts needed to be replaced when they didn't. Figure he charged for the replacement part but put the old one back on and sold the new part so he could pocket the money."

"Was this going on for a while?"

"Not long. Nate runs a tight ship, and we figured out pretty quickly that something was off. We have a reputation to uphold." Marty shrugged. "He was an ex-con, but Nate gave the guy a chance. Guess it just wasn't meant to be."

"You hire ex-cons?" This time the man directed his question to Nate.

Nate nodded. "I figure everyone deserves a second chance. It doesn't always work out, but we've never had something like this happen before."

"He must have had some help."

Marty grunted. "No doubt some of those dudes that kept coming around the shop when he was supposed to be working."

"Yeah, I would agree with that," Nate told the man. "But I don't know who they were."

Throughout the conversation, he'd kept his gaze pinned on the burning building. Slowly but surely the flames were dying out. The heat radiating off the building also began to ebb away. The charred rubble of the building represented more than just the loss of a business. This had been his dad's dream, the last thing they had worked to build together. In fact, it had been at this garage that Mike Proctor had the heart attack which eventually led to his death.

"I'm so sorry, Dad," Nate whispered as he looked up to the black night sky.

As the flames faded away, so did the crowd. Soon it was just him, Marty, the firefighters and a handful of cops. Nate let out a weary sigh as he envisioned what lay ahead of him in the coming days. A small voice told him to dump it all, jump in his truck and leave everything behind. The heartbreak, the pain, the ruins of his life. Go start over somewhere else. Someplace the memories didn't follow him everywhere he went.

His phone rang, and when he lifted it to see the screen, he frowned. *Crystal.* He didn't want to talk to her right then. No doubt she was calling for the same reason the sheriff had.

Nate took a few steps away from Marty and the firefighter. "Hello?"

"Nate? Nate? Is that you? Are you okay?"

"I'm fine." He kicked at the ground as he stood with his head bent. "I wasn't at my house in Collingsworth."

"You know what happened already?" The tone of her voice edged up. "You should have called to let me know you were okay. Where are you?"

Nate could hear the hurt in her words. "I'm in Sanford. I decided to stay the night here when things ran long at the garage."

"I've been going out of my mind with worry. Why didn't you call me?"

"I'm sorry, Crys. I'm dealing with some stuff here in Sanford, too. I didn't realize what was going on in Collingsworth until the sheriff called a little bit ago."

A couple of beats of silence passed. "I'm just glad you're okay."

"Me, too." Nate rubbed his forehead with his fingertips. "Listen, I'll give you a call when I'm back in Collingsworth. Should be sometime tomorrow." He could tell she didn't want to end the conversation, but he couldn't deal with her right then. Their relationship was one more struggle for him. She wanted so much more than he could give. It wasn't fair to allow things to continue when he knew there was no future for them. Though sweet and cute, Crystal just wasn't what his heart longed for.

But he'd deal with that problem another day. Right then, he needed to focus on the problems at hand. After that, he would try to figure out how to pick up the pieces of his life for the third time.

ᠭᡐᠬᠥ

The plane came to a stop with a jerk. Immediately people began to stand and reach for the overhead bins. Lily Collingsworth remained in her seat, her gaze on the view beyond the window next to her. There wasn't anything really worth looking at—just the huge buildings that made up the Minneapolis/St. Paul International Airport—but she didn't want some kind soul to stop to let her out. She was seated in first class and could presumably have exited rather quickly, but the fourteen-hour trip had been exhausting for her, and she didn't trust her legs to have to work too quickly. The last thing she wanted was to stumble or fall in front of an audience.

The door didn't open right away, so it took almost fifteen minutes for the noise in the aisle to subside. Lily glanced over to see that the remaining line was made up of just a few stragglers now. She reached for her purse under the seat in front of her and slowly stood. One of the flight attendants approached her.

"Is this your bag?" he asked as he reached into the overhead compartment.

"Yes." Lily gave him a smile as he handed it down to her. He pulled up the handle and then stepped back to allow her to step into the aisle. She took the handle from him. "Thank you for your help."

"You're welcome."

Moving carefully between the few rows of seats that stood between her and the exit of the plane, Lily prayed she could make it up the long walkway to the main terminal. Once there, hopefully the help she'd requested would be waiting to take her to where she could claim the remainder of her luggage. Thankfully, she'd cleared customs in Chicago on a layover so there would be no delay for that. And then it would be the final three-hour ride to Collingsworth.

With slow measured steps, Lily made her way up the walkway and entered the terminal. Crowds of people milled around, and she took a minute to survey the area and orient herself. She approached the airline desk.

"My name is Lily Collingsworth, and I had requested transport from here to the baggage claim," she told the woman behind the counter.

She saw the woman's gaze drop as if to see why she needed the transport, but the large counter blocked her view. It wouldn't have mattered anyway. Lily knew most people looked at her and didn't see why she needed aid. And most of the time, if she was careful, she didn't require it, but today, after such a long trip, Lily knew enough about her body to not push it any further.

Though the woman didn't seem overly sympathetic, she did pick up the phone and make the request. Within a few minutes, a cart with room for four people pulled up. Lily settled into the back of it with her carry-on and purse and told the driver where she needed to go. She looked straight forward so as not to meet the wondering glances of the people they passed.

With the end of her journey so close now, Lily just wanted it to be over.

As they left the secured area and approached the baggage carousel, Lily looked around for the person who was to drive her to Collingsworth. Because she knew the length of the trip would tire her, she hadn't bothered with trying to rent a car to drive herself. Instead, she'd paid handsomely for someone to chauffeur her home. One of the benefits of having money.

After the driver of the cart let her off with her bags, Lily looked around at the people gathered there. It didn't take long to spot the person holding the placard that read "Lily C."

She approached the woman dressed in a chauffeur's uniform and smiled. "Hi. I'm Lily."

The woman lowered the placard and held out her hand. "I'm Melissa. I'll be driving you to Collingsworth today."

"I'm very glad to see you," Lily told her. "Would you be able to help me with my bags?"

Lily had specified when she'd made the arrangements that she wanted a woman driver and also that the person be willing to help her with the luggage. Melissa nodded and immediately went to get a cart on which to load the bags as they came off the carousel.

Forty-five minutes later, the luggage was stowed in the trunk of the car and they were on their way.

It wasn't long into the trip when Lily began to feel the exhaustion pulling at her. The tiredness didn't come as any surprise, and it had, in fact, been the reason she'd requested a female driver. She figured she'd likely fall asleep at some point during the drive and felt more secure having a woman present with her in the car than she would have a man.

She leaned forward and spoke to Melissa. "I've had a long day, so I'm going to try to sleep a little. Please wake me when we get to Collingsworth, and I'll direct you to where I need to go."

"I understand, Miss Collingsworth." Melissa met her gaze in the rearview mirror and smiled.

Letting out a sigh, Lily settled back against the seat and closed her eyes. She didn't immediately fall asleep though. Too many thoughts swirled through her mind. While she was relieved to be coming home to Collingsworth, Lily knew the days ahead were not going to be easy. Her family still didn't know the reasons why she'd left almost three years earlier. No doubt they would have plenty of questions for her. They were questions she hadn't wanted to deal with before, but now she would. At least she had more informed answers now than she'd had back then. And she'd done a lot of maturing over the past three years. Leaving had forced her to take responsibility for herself, among other things. And she planned to continue to do so even though she was returning to the manor and her family there.

And Nate. She had no idea how he'd been over the past three years. It had been important to her that she sever their bond completely when she left. Her best friend—the one person she'd kept in regular contact with—had rarely mentioned him, and during her sporadic conversations with her older sister, Jessa, over the years, Lily had never asked anything about him. And she was returning home with no expectation that they would pick up where they'd left off. In fact, she knew it wouldn't be possible.

⨯ Chapter Two ⨯

MISS Collingsworth?"

Lily woke to the sound of her name, quickly realizing she'd fallen asleep in mid-thought. Straightening, she looked out the front window to see the town of Collingsworth looming ahead.

"You can just continue on this road through town and then turn right when we get to the highway."

Pressing a hand to her stomach, Lily took several deep breaths. Nerves fluttered in her belly. She'd taken another page from Cami's book and planned to show up unannounced. Doing it that way had given her an out. If she decided to change her plans, no one was expecting her. Because even though Lily knew coming home was the right decision, a lot of difficult conversations lay ahead.

It didn't take long for the car to pass through the town and reach the highway. "You can take a right just up there."

Melissa slowed the car and turned onto the driveway which led to the manor. Lily found herself leaning forward to catch a glimpse of her home. A blanket of relief settled over her as they followed the final bend in the driveway, bringing the manor into view.

"What a beautiful house," Melissa said as she brought the car to a stop in front of the steps.

"Yes, it is," Lily agreed. She grabbed her purse from the seat beside her and opened the door. "If you want to just hang on a minute, I'm sure there are some men here who will help carry my bags in."

Without waiting for the woman to respond, Lily headed for the front door. She grasped the door handle and paused for a second before opening it and stepping into the foyer. Immediately the savory scent of dinner greeted her. Something along the lines of a pot roast, if her senses were still accurate. She heard the murmur of conversation coming from the kitchen and moved in that direction.

"Lily!"

Before she could even respond, Lily found herself in the middle of a tight hug. Tears sprang to her eyes, and she sagged against the arms that held her.

Home at last.

"Are you okay, sweetie?" Laurel's voice was laced with concern. "Here, come sit down."

Lily allowed herself to be led to an empty seat at the table. Through damp eyes, she took in those present. Everyone but Jessa, and there was a woman she didn't recognize with a mass of curly blonde hair and a curious expression on her face.

"You got luggage, sis?" Will asked.

Lily looked at him and nodded. "Outside with the driver."

All the men left the table and headed out of the kitchen.

"Why didn't you tell us you were coming home?" Violet asked. Her expression turned dark. "And, for that matter, why haven't you been in better contact with us? We've been worried."

Lily reached out to touch her sister's arm. "I'm sorry. I needed to work through some things."

"And it took you three years?" This time it was Cami that asked. "Although I guess I'm one to talk, eh?"

"True," Laurel agreed.

Lily smiled. She'd missed them more than she'd realized.

"Your timing is great though, since Cami and Josh are still here." The blonde woman gave her a friendly smile.

There was an increase in noise as the men came back in with the luggage, but they bypassed the kitchen and went right upstairs.

"Where's Jessa?" Her oldest sister's absence, when everyone else including her husband was present, concerned Lily.

"She's on bed rest," Laurel said.

"Bed rest?" Lily asked. "When did that happen?"

"She's been on bed rest for several weeks because of some bleeding, contractions and blood pressure issues," Violet explained. "Amy came to help out until the baby is born."

"And then Will fell in love with her, and the rest is history," Laurel added with a grin.

The blonde woman—Amy—blushed. "Yeah, guess I'll be sticking around for a bit longer."

"I'm sure Will's hoping it's for longer than just a bit," Cami said. "And I'm hoping you're around for longer than a bit, too, Lily."

Lily nodded. "I'm home for good."

The men came back into the kitchen before Lily could say anything more. Lance came over and gave her a hug. "You need to go upstairs and see Jessa. She's almost ready to come down here, but I can't let that happen."

Lily needed to see Jessa, too. She just hoped her legs would cooperate. When she stood, her legs shook a little. She glanced at Lance. "Will you come up with me?"

Lance nodded. "Sure."

Lily waited for Lance to join her. As they approached the bottom of the stairs, she reached for his arm with one hand as she grasped the banister with the other. Lance immediately stilled and looked down at her.

"What's wrong, Lily?" Concern was evident on his face.

"It's a long story. I plan to share it, but not right now. Most days I'm fine, but my body is reacting to the very long day it has just had. I need a little help."

His brow furrowed but even though he looked like he wanted to ask more questions, he just covered her hand with his and began to slowly climb the stairs. Lily was thankful for his understanding and patience. Once they reached the door of his and Jessa's bedroom, she eased her grasp on his arm, determined to make the steps to Jessa's bed on her own.

"Lily!" Jessa held out her arms as soon as she spotted her.

As quickly as she could, Lily moved toward her oldest sister and sank into her embrace, mindful of the mound of her belly. Lily's tears flowed as she hugged the woman who had been as close to a mother as she'd had.

"I've prayed every day for you to come home." As she sat back from their embrace, Jessa took Lily's face in her hands, her thumbs grazing the wetness on her cheeks. "I've missed you so much."

"I have a lot to tell you, but not right now," Lily said. "I just want to enjoy being home."

"Come sit up here with me." Jessa patted the bed on the other side of her.

Lily settled down on the bed and placed her hand lightly on Jessa's stomach. "Another baby!"

"It took long enough, but we're finally going to get our boy."

Lily rested her head on Jessa's shoulder. "I'm so happy

for you." It seemed like life had been good for her siblings. Will had found love. Jessa was pregnant. Part of her didn't want to share what had been happening with her, she really didn't want to bring them down.

Once again, Lily felt tiredness tugging at her and tried to stifle a yawn. She pushed herself to a sitting position. "It's been a super long day, and if I stay here on this bed much longer, Lance will have to find someplace else to sleep. I've been up since about two o'clock in the morning your time."

Jessa brushed a hand over her hair. "We'll talk later. I'm not going anywhere. Come find me when you're up and about tomorrow."

"I will." Lily pressed a kiss to her cheek. "Love you."

Lily spotted Lance as she walked out of the bedroom. He sat on a chair in their sitting room, arms propped on his thighs, head bent down.

He looked up and smiled. "Ready to go back downstairs?"

"Yes, for a few minutes. To say goodnight."

Lance once again supported her as they slowly walked down to the main floor. As they moved off the last step, he turned toward her. His gaze was serious as he looked down at her. "It's MS, isn't it?"

Though his voice was low, the words were clear. Lily stared at him in shock. "How did you know?"

Lance's head tipped as sadness spread across his face. "I had a friend in high school whose mom had it. Something about how you moved threw me back in time."

"It's usually not this bad. I've been busy preparing for the move back, and the long day has just made it worse than it normally would be. A good night's sleep and some low activity days will help me out."

Lance nodded. "Well, most of us will be off to church in the morning, but don't feel you need to come. Jessa stays home, and I usually stay with her. Tomorrow night Cami and Josh will be giving a concert at the church, so you're back in time for that."

"I'd love to go." Lily moved toward the kitchen with Lance. The other family members were still gathered there in deep conversation, but they all looked up as Lily and Lance walked in. "I hate to show up and then crash, but it's been one very long day, and I'm beat."

She quickly gave hugs to everyone before heading back upstairs. Lance went with her once again, promising that he wouldn't say anything about her diagnosis until she had a chance to share it herself.

"We're here for you," Lance assured her. "Don't go running off again."

Lily gave him a tired smile. "No chance of that. I'm home for good now."

Knowing she probably wouldn't have the energy to unpack her suitcases when she arrived, Lily had packed the things she needed for the night in her carry-on. It didn't take long to get ready for bed, and this time no thoughts were strong enough to keep her awake.

∽◈∾

Nate pulled to a stop in front of the manor. He was very grateful for the Collingsworths' generous offer of a place to stay given the current condition of his home. The sheriff, who also happened to be Violet's husband, had extended the invitation to stay at the manor after he'd gotten back to Collingsworth the day after the fires. He could have gone to a motel, but he was certain the isolation would have done a number on his mind. Instead, he was surrounded by people sympathetic to his situation, but who still gave him the space he needed.

He took the front steps two at a time, eager to put the day behind him. He'd had to go back to Sanford to meet with the man who was leading the investigation into the fire. After that meeting, he'd stayed to have dinner with Marty and his family. He was concerned about his employees. He didn't want them to be out of work, but there was no way he could continue to pay them without the garage there being functional. It weighed heavily on him even though Marty had assured him that *God's got this*. Nate wished he shared his employee's confidence.

Staying at the manor had freed up some of his money since they refused to take any pay from him. So the money he'd have had to spend on a motel, he planned to give to Marty to help him and his family out until the man could find another job.

"Evening," Nate said as he rounded the corner to the kitchen to find most the Collingsworths gathered around the table there.

"How's it going?" the sheriff—or Dean, as he'd requested Nate call him—asked.

"Well, as expected, all signs point to arson, but they haven't been able to find the guys responsible yet."

"They'll show up eventually." Dean spoke with more confidence than Nate felt about the situation. He hoped the sheriff was right. "Those types of guys can't stay hidden very long. They're not smart enough."

As Dean spoke, Nate caught Laurel and Violet exchanging glances before looking at him. "Everything okay here?"

Again, they looked at each briefly, but this time Violet spoke. "Um, we had no idea this was going to happen, but Lily arrived home tonight."

Feeling as if he'd just been kicked in the gut, Nate braced a hand on the wall beside him. "Lily? She's here?"

Laurel nodded. "She arrived an hour ago, but she's already gone up to her room."

"Well, I'll get my things together and go to the motel." There was no way she would want him around, he was certain of that.

Lance stood and came to him, laying a hand on his shoulder. "Actually, I think it would be good if you stayed.

There's plenty of room here. I don't understand all the events that have transpired over the past few days, but I feel that God has brought us all together in this place for a reason. We want to support you through this difficult time. God only knows why Lily has come home now, but I don't think it's necessary for you to leave."

Nate glanced around at the others seated there. Each of them was nodding their head, apparently in agreement with Lance. "Well, I'll stay for tonight and then let her decide what she wants me to do."

"Fair enough," Lance said. "I guess we should also tell you that we didn't let her know that you were staying here yet. She was pretty tired from the flight, but I'll make sure she knows tomorrow."

Nate was at a loss for words. *Lily? Here?*

Just when his life had completely fallen apart again, she showed back up. A knot formed in his stomach. The pain of her leaving three years ago and then not communicating with him at all still lingered. He had wondered how it would be to see her again after all this time. But right then, facing the realization that it was going to happen sooner rather than later, Nate wasn't sure he was ready for it.

"Guess I'm going to head up and crash. I'm running on about two hours sleep out of the past forty-eight."

"Once again let me say how sorry we are for what's happened," Lance said. "Be sure and let us know if there's anything we can do to help."

"Giving me a place to stay has been plenty of help. I appreciate it a lot." He hoped his weariness didn't show too much as he smiled at the group. "See you in the morning."

They said goodnight as he turned to leave. He paused just outside the kitchen. Laurel's voice carried to where he stood.

"Lance, are you sure it's a good idea to have them both here?"

"Trust me on this one." Lance's voice was firm. "I believe it's God's timing."

Nate reached out to grip the banister of the stairs and began the climb to the second floor. The door to the room that Lily had once used was closed where it hadn't been up until that point. He hesitated for a moment before turning in the direction of his room.

Though he felt considerably better after a shower, the headache that had been pulsing at his temples earlier had turned into a full on throbbing one.

Once hitting town earlier, he'd stopped and bought a few more clothes and some toiletries since all he had left were the things he'd taken with him to Sanford. He dug through the bag for something to sleep in and found the bottle of painkillers he'd bought as well. After getting a glass of water from the bathroom, he popped a couple of them and then sank down on the bed.

For the first time, the enormity of his loss struck him. Everything he'd had was gone. The photos of his mom and dad. He had some of the pictures scanned onto his computer, but not all of them. There were digital photos that he'd saved on the computer as well. Thankfully he'd used an online back-up system so all his business records and other personal documents and the pictures he did have were safe.

But there would be no replacing the things of more sentimental value. The gifts his mom had chosen for him. Or the ones Lily had given him. Even the engagement ring she'd returned to him was gone now. Like a sentimental fool, he'd kept it in the nightstand next to his bed instead of the fireproof safe or a safety deposit box.

He pressed his fingers against his forehead. *Nothing.* That's what he had. *Absolutely nothing.* For the life of him, he couldn't figure out exactly what he'd done to deserve all of this heartache. God must have it out for him.

Even though he still had the garage in Collingsworth, it was going to be shut down for a couple of weeks. The fire had never fully engaged, but there had been enough damage done that he needed to have it repaired before continuing on with his business.

He leaned forward, grasping his head in his hands. The temptation to just pack up and leave was stronger than ever. Particularly now that he knew Lily was back. She'd probably thank her lucky stars that she'd left him when she did.

Pull yourself together, son. Trust God for the strength to go on.

The words in the voice of his father came to him so clearly he actually lifted his head to look around the room. Though his father had been gone for almost two years, so much of what he'd taught Nate had lingered on. Particularly the part about going on in spite of the difficult circumstances. If anyone had known about that, it had been his father. He'd nursed a wife as she battled a terminal illness, and had managed to build up a business that had been respected throughout the community. The least Nate could do in his father's honor was to pick himself up from this and go on.

Though it was barely nine o'clock, Nate crawled under the covers and snapped off the light on the nightstand. He set the alarm on his phone and finally allowed the exhaustion that he'd been fighting for hours to overtake him.

❧ Chapter Three ❧

"CAN you come to my place for lunch?" Crystal asked him when the service was over the next day. "I put on a chicken before I left."

Nate nodded. She'd been so patient with his distraction over the past couple of days since the fire. "I'll meet you there."

When someone stopped him, she continued on to the main doors of the church and disappeared outside. A few more people paused to offer their sympathies over the loss of his home and business. He appreciated their support but was eager to get out of the church. Too many were asking what his plans were, but since he didn't know anything yet, he really didn't want to keep being asked about it. Sometime in the next week he'd figured things out, but for now, he was taking it a day at a time.

Though he'd tried not to look around for her, it hadn't been hard to notice that Lily wasn't with her family when they had filed into the pews of the church that morning. Nate still wondered at the wisdom of staying at the manor with

27

her there, but until he had a chance to talk with her, he would heed Lance's advice to stay put.

He pulled his truck to a stop outside Crystal's small house and sat for a few moments before getting out. If he'd still been with Lily, the first thing he'd have done after receiving Dean's call would have been to call and let her know he was okay. That had not been the case with Crystal, and that alone spoke loudly of how differently he viewed the two relationships. Since then, he'd been toying with the idea of ending things. But that was before hearing about Lily. Now it would just seem like he was breaking up with her because of Lily's return. Though it couldn't be further from the truth, with things the way they were it would be hard to get her to believe that.

She immediately answered his knock on her back door. He stepped into the kitchen, enjoying the smell of roast chicken that lingered in the air.

"Smells delicious."

"Thanks. I hope it tastes delicious, too. Want something to drink?" She busied herself with the salad fixings on the counter. "There are cold sodas in the fridge or water if you want."

Nate opened the fridge and grabbed a can of his favorite soda. He popped the top and took a long drink. As he watched her work, Nate realized that she hadn't met his gaze since he'd walked in. Did she know Lily was back? Was that making her uncomfortable?

Before he could say anything, a timer went off. She grabbed a couple of pot holders and pulled the chicken from the oven.

"Do you want me to carve that?" Nate asked as he set his soda down on the counter. "I think I could manage not to butcher it too much."

"Sure." She pulled a knife from the drawer and laid it next to the roast chicken, still not looking at him. "You can put it on that platter."

They worked without talking, but thankfully she had music playing to fill the silence so he didn't feel compelled to strike up a conversation. Usually, Crystal was the one who chattered about a variety of things when they were together, but today there was only silence from her.

Once they were seated at the table, she bent her head and said grace. He noticed once prayer was done, she didn't put much food on her plate. Finally, he set his fork and knife down and said, "What's wrong? You've barely said two words since I arrived."

Still not looking at him, she set her silverware down as well. She took a sip of her drink and then finally looked at him. "I was going to wait until after lunch, but I don't think it will make much difference now."

"What are you talking about?" Nate pushed his plate forward and rested his arms on the table.

Crystal took a deep breath and lifted her chin. "I knew all about your relationship with Lily before we started dating. I knew you'd been engaged to her, and it had ended suddenly just before she left town. Naively, I assumed I could be the one to help you heal and move on from her. I knew it might take time, but I figured that eventually you'd see how much I loved you and would love me like that in return."

A sick feeling settled in the pit of his stomach. "I'm sorry."

She held up a hand. "Let me finish. About six months into our relationship, I finally had to admit it wasn't going to be the easy change I had thought it would be. It was then I told myself that if I didn't feel your emotions were fully engaged in our relationship when Lily came back, I would end things." She paused then shrugged. "So here we are. Lily's back, and it's time to end things."

The news had certainly traveled fast. "Crys--"

Again she stopped him, this time with a shake of her head. "I knew this day would come. I've known for a few months now that there was no hope for us, but I held on anyway. Hoping for a miracle, I guess."

"I'm sorry," he said again.

"It's not your fault. I should have ended things a lot sooner. And I know you feel the same way, but probably didn't want to let me down."

Nate couldn't argue with her. "I wish I could have been what you wanted...needed in this relationship."

A sad smile lifted the corners of her lips. "I wish you could have been, too. But I ignored all the signs and made things more difficult on myself. I just want you to know I understand. You can't force yourself to feel something you don't. You never told me lies about loving me or talked about the future in such a way that you dragged out that hope in me. I chose to hang on longer than I should have."

"You're a beautiful, sweet, caring woman, and I wish things would have worked out differently." Nate's appetite had long since fled. "Please know that there has been nothing between Lily and me in all the time we've been together. And there won't be. She made it clear things were over for us when she left. I haven't even seen her since she got back." He let out a long sigh. "For some reason my heart is just not ready to move on yet, even though I know it's been almost three years."

"You've had a lot to deal with over the years since she left. I know my pursuing you hasn't helped give you the space you need to heal from it all. I don't know how things will be for you now with Lily back here, but I hope you find some closure and peace in your heart."

"Thank you," Nate said, wishing at that moment that he had been able to give Crystal what she'd needed in their relationship. She'd been so good to him, and though he'd try to give her what he could, he had always known it wasn't enough.

"Don't feel you have to finish your lunch." She waved at his half-empty plate. "I just didn't want to do this out in public at a restaurant." She pushed back from the table and stood.

Nate got to his feet and reached to pull her into a quick hug. "Take care of yourself."

A tear slid down her cheek, but still she smiled at him. "I will. And you do the same."

He'd thought ending the relationship would have made him feel better, but as Nate walked to his truck, all he felt was heartsick and weary. Somehow he had to shore up his defenses and pull the broken parts of his life back together. Sitting in his truck, he pulled out his phone and called his buddy, Stan. He had no desire to return to the manor yet knowing that Lily was there.

"Why don't you come on over and watch the race?" Stan suggested. "Pretty sure your guy's not going to win, but you can celebrate with me when mine does."

Nate chuckled at his friend's taunt. "I'll be right over. Want me to stop for anything on the way?"

"Nope. We went to the store last night and bought a bunch of stuff. Just bring yourself and be prepared to spend some time holding the baby. I promised Ella she could take a nap, so we're on baby duty if he decides not to sleep as well."

Nate figured there were worse things in life than watching a NASCAR race while holding a baby. "See you in a few minutes."

◈◈◈

Lily followed Amy and Will as they walked down the aisle of the church. Though she'd missed the service that morning, she had felt much better and had wanted to attend Josh and Cami's concert. As they filed into a pew, she fought the urge to look around. No doubt people were curious about her reappearance. But mostly she didn't want to see Nate just yet, and she was fairly certain he was present somewhere in the sanctuary.

When Lance had told her about Nate's recent troubles and the fact that he was staying at the manor, she'd been shocked. Though she'd known she'd have to face him sooner or later, she hadn't figured on him being quite so close. It was pretty apparent from his absence from the manor all day that he wasn't all that eager to see her either. Not that she blamed him.

It had been for his own good. Now more than ever she was glad she'd ended things because the last thing he would have needed would have been her problems on top of his. She had been surprised—though she knew she shouldn't have been—at the shaft of pain she'd felt when Violet had told her he'd been dating a woman named Crystal.

Lily hoped that she was good for him. It was only now, looking back after almost three years apart, that she could see the relationship she'd had with Nate hadn't been a real healthy one.

"Have you been to many of their concerts?"

Lily pulled her thoughts back to the present and turned to see Amy watching her. "I've been to two, and they were great. I'm really looking forward to tonight."

"This is my first one here, but I always go to the ones they have in Dallas when they come to visit for Christmas. It's become a holiday tradition at our church."

"Are you planning to move back there? Or are you staying here now?"

Amy glanced over at Will and smiled. "Well, it's kind of looking like I'm going to be staying here for the time being. I don't have a job to go back to anymore, so I'm just going to hang around and see what happens."

Lily was curious about the young woman who had captured Will's heart. When she'd left, he'd still been struggling with his roles of widower and single father. It was so good to see a smile back on his face and the way his eyes lit up when he looked at Amy. Seeing her siblings in good relationships was going to have to be enough for her.

That first night after her diagnosis she'd spent hours reading everything she could find about MS, and it quickly became apparent to her that she was going to face this journey alone. Nate had often spoken of the stress his father had been under being a caregiver for his wife during her illness while also trying to run a business and being there for his son. Knowing that her condition would only get worse as the years went by, Lily had made the heartbreaking decision to spare Nate from having to care for her in the way his father had cared for his mother. She couldn't stay around Collingsworth after ending things with him, and even as she sat there today, she knew it had been the right decision to leave.

Noise from the center aisle drew Lily's attention. Before she could stop herself, she glanced to see what was going on. A group of young people were laughing as they filed into a row near the front. Her gaze moved to the row behind them, and her breath snagged when she saw Nate sitting at the far end of the pew. His head was bent, but as if sensing her watching him, he looked up and his gaze swung in her direction.

When their gazes met, Lily realized that no matter how much she thought she'd moved past Nate Proctor, her heart cried out for him. Fearful of what he might read on her face, she gave him a small smile before turning back around to where Cami and Josh were taking their places on the stage.

Lily had thought she was over Nate. But all it had taken was one look, and she was back to where she'd been three years ago. Part of the reason she'd felt ready to come back to Collingsworth was because she thought her heartbreak over Nate had finally healed. Unfortunately, it appeared that was not the case, but it was too late now to do anything about it. She was home, and she'd just have to pray that she was strong enough to be able to deal with him. He had moved on, and now she needed to do that as well.

Thankfully Josh and Cami's concert got underway, and she found herself relaxing and enjoying their performance. Most of the songs were familiar. Some she recognized as new songs they'd written together. Even though she'd been away, she'd been sure to keep up with their album releases.

As the applause faded after one of their songs near what Lily assumed was the end of their concert, Josh stepped forward. Cami stayed behind him, mic held at her waist.

"One thing Cami and I have learned in our own lives and as we've spoken to people at our concerts is that we all face struggles. So often we feel alone. We think that friends, family and even God have abandoned us to our pain. I know that feeling. I've been there. Cami's been there. And tonight I'm feeling there are some of you here that feel that way. This song was one that often came to my mind during those times when I felt so low that I didn't think I could go any lower. It's a reminder to each of us that we aren't alone. That Jesus does truly care."

As the music began, Lily closed her eyes and listened as Josh sang the opening to the song.

> Does Jesus care when my heart is pained
> Too deeply for mirth or song,
> As the burdens press and the cares distress,
> And the way grows weary and long.

As Josh's voice faded away, Cami began to sing the next verse.

> Does Jesus care when my way is dark
> With a nameless dread and fear?
> As the daylight fades into deep night shades,
> Does He care enough to be near?
> Together they sang,
> Oh yes, He cares, I know He cares,
> His heart is touched with my grief;
> When the days are weary, the long nights dreary,
> I know my Savior cares.

Lily's heart clenched. That nameless dread and fear had plagued her so much during those first days in London when it was just her alone with her diagnosis. And her daylight had faded into the deepest of night shades. It had been at the darkest of those moments when she had cried for healing from the disease that had taken up residence in her body.

Does Jesus care when I've tried and failed
To resist some temptation strong;
When for my deep grief there is no relief,
Though my tears flow all the night long?

There was a change in key and Josh sang,

Does Jesus care when I've said 'goodbye'
to the dearest on earth to me.
And my sad heart aches till it nearly breaks,
is it aught to him? Does He see?
Oh yes, He cares, I know He cares,
His heart is touched with my grief;
When the days are weary, the long nights dreary,
I know my Savior cares.

The song was familiar to her as it had been on one of their earliest releases, and she'd played it many times. *Oh yes, He cares.* It was one of the things that had gotten her through those early days. Even though she hadn't opened the Bible and sought comfort there at the time, the words of the songs Josh and Cami sang had kept her from sinking completely into the darkness after her diagnosis. Eventually, the Bible had become her place of solace, but it had been the music that had drawn her there.

Once the concert was over, people surged to the foyer to where Josh and Cami had gone as the pastor closed the evening in prayer. Lily moved more slowly, trying to keep from looking in Nate's direction. Sooner or later they were going to meet. She just wasn't sure she wanted it to be in public with the whole church looking on. There were probably very few people in the church that didn't know about their history.

Several people came up to her and welcomed her home as she made her way with Will and Amy to the foyer of the church. Lily had anticipated a period of awkwardness and curiosity as people wondered about her absence for the past few years.

"Lily!"

She turned in time to be tackled in a tight hug. The site of familiar red curls had her returning the hug instantly. Before she could say anything, the young woman pushed back from their embrace and held her at arm's length. "I can't believe you're finally home. You're not allowed to leave ever again."

Lily smiled. "Hi, Meggy. It's good to see you, too."

Meg's hands slid down to clasp hers, her brow furrowing. "I'm so glad you're home for good."

"I am, too. It was time."

Meg nodded. "I thought it might be after our last conversation." She pulled her close for a hug again. "I just can't tell you how wonderful it is to have you home. I've missed you so much."

"Come out to the manor for a visit," Lily said.

"I will. And if you need anything at all, let me know." Meg was the only person who had known about her diagnosis almost from the start. She had been a rock once she'd understood why Lily had fled Collingsworth.

As they stepped apart once more, Lily's gaze went past Meg to a man who stood just behind her friend, a patient look on his face. Meg must have realized where Lily's attention was because she quickly turned and reach out to take the man's hand.

"Lily, I'd like you to meet Andrew. Andrew, this is my best friend, Lily Collingsworth."

Lily shook the hand Andrew held out to her, curious about this man who had managed to capture Meg's somewhat flighty attention. She'd heard all about him during their phone calls, so it was nice to finally meet him.

They made small talk for a few minutes before Meg glanced at her boyfriend. "Well, I hate to run, but Andrew has an early morning tomorrow, so he needs to get home. He's my ride."

"I'm hoping my ride is ready to go soon, too," Lily said.

After Meg and Andrew had left, Lily looked around for Will and Amy. She spotted them standing at the product table and knew they wouldn't be leaving for a little while yet. The crowd of people was starting to close in on her, and she knew that if she was going to have to wait around, she'd rather do it outside.

She took a deep breath as she stepped into the warm night air. Since it was just after nine, the sun had already begun to set, leaving behind a darkening twilight sky. Lily moved off to the side and sank down onto the stone bench there. She pulled out her phone and opened up her social media app.

"Hello, Lily."

A rush of warmth moved through her. It had been three years since she'd last heard his voice, though he had rarely called her that. Usually it had been *Lily-belle* or *baby*. But those days were gone. From now on, it would only and forever be *Lily*.

∽ *Chapter Four* ∾

LILY looked up to meet his dark brown eyes. His expression was guarded, but she could see the signs of exhaustion on his face. Her heart clenched as she recalled all he'd been through since she'd left.

"Hi, Nate."

He wore a pair of dark blue jeans and a white polo shirt. He'd never been one for dressing up and when they'd gotten engaged, he'd made her promise he wouldn't have to wear a tux at the wedding. Of course, that was now a moot point. She couldn't help but notice that the flecks of gray in his hair were more plentiful than they'd been three years ago. He wasn't even thirty-five yet, but life's challenges were taking their toll on him.

Though his stance—hands on hips, feet braced apart—was distancing, Lily wanted to wrap her arms around him and feel his around her. But again...that was no longer going to be part of her present or future. She'd made sure of that.

"Would you like a ride home?"

His words surprised her. She wondered how his girlfriend

might feel about the offer. Regardless, it was very tempting. She was tired and getting home was very appealing, but since he was with someone now, she didn't feel right about accepting.

"Thank you, but I think I'll just wait for Amy and Will." She looked past him, searching for the woman who had laid claim to his heart once she'd set it free. "I wouldn't want to cause trouble for you."

Nate stared at her for a moment then said, "There's no one to cause trouble with. I'm heading to the manor now and thought maybe you'd rather head home than hang out here."

No one? The words contradicted the information she'd been given earlier. If something had happened, it had happened recently because as far as Violet had known, he was still with Crystal. "If you're sure..."

There was still no change to his expression. "I wouldn't have offered if I wasn't sure."

Don't do it, the voice in her head warned. But she told herself that it was for the sake of her health. "Then in that case, yes, I would like a ride back to the manor."

He gave a short nod of his head and looked out to the parking lot. Lily grabbed her purse and stood, hoping her legs wouldn't give out on her. In this case it had less to do with the MS than it did the nerves that had suddenly overtaken her body.

Nate gestured to the far side of the parking lot. "I'm parked just over there."

Though it was tempting to slide her hand into the crook of his arm, Lily gripped the strap of her purse tightly instead. All those things that she'd once taken for granted as part of their relationship were no longer hers. And that was because of the decision she'd made, no matter how heartbreaking it had been, and one she needed to stand by.

Could they be friends? She didn't know, but if they were both going to be staying at the manor for the time being, they would need to be able to be around each other without making everyone else uncomfortable. This drive out to the manor would be a good start.

Once at the truck, he opened the door for her. In the past he would have at least held out his hand to help her or, more often than not, he would have lifted her up onto the seat. This time Lily gripped the handle above the door and leveraged herself in. Once she settled into the seat, he shut the door. Immediately the scent of his cologne enveloped her. It was an oh-so-familiar fragrance that lingered in the truck even when he wasn't inside it. One she'd often bought for him as a gift. Had Crystal been the one to give him more bottles of it after the last one she'd given him had run out?

The cab of the truck seemed to shrink as he climbed behind the wheel and pulled his door closed. Without looking at her, he started up the ignition and backed out of the parking spot. Lily took her phone out and texted a quick message to Amy so they wouldn't wait around wondering where she was.

Caught a ride home. See you later.

Lily slid her phone back into her purse. "Just letting Amy know I got a ride home, so they aren't looking for me."

"Good idea."

Nate had never been one for talking a lot, and early on Lily had learned to accept his silences and not try to fill it with chatter, though she realized now that more often than not she had. But this silence was awkward and loaded with so many unasked and unanswered questions.

"I'm sorry to hear about your dad," Lily said. "And about what happened to your home and the garage in Sanford."

Nate glanced at her. "Thanks."

Lily knew that although Nate's dad had always treated her well, he hadn't believed her to be the right person for Nate. He hadn't said it to her directly, but Nate had conveyed some of it. She was too young for him. Too impulsive. And worse,

Nate's dad felt that because of the seven-year age gap, she viewed Nate more like a father figure than a boyfriend. Nate's mom, however, had always been very sweet to her. She'd died a year after they'd started dating, so Lily hadn't known her too well, but she'd seen the toll her illness had taken on Nate and his dad.

"Are you going to rebuild in Sanford?"

"Not sure yet," Nate said. "I'd like to, simply because I have some good guys there. But I also don't expect them to wait around for me to rebuild since it may take a while."

The sky continued to darken as they left the lights of the town behind. Their times driving together had always been Lily's favorite. It was one of the few times she'd had his undivided attention. From the time they'd started dating when she'd turned eighteen, she'd always had to share him with his mom and dad and his job. Often she'd felt like she was the last thing on his priority list and if not for her effort, they might have spent even less time together. Knowing how important his job and his dad had been to him, Lily knew she couldn't burden him with her diagnosis as well.

The remainder of the trip passed in silence. Lily didn't know what else to talk about, and he wasn't pursuing conversation either. Thankfully the drive to the manor didn't take too long. Once he'd pulled to a stop in front of the garage, Lily turned to him.

"Thank you for the ride." She had opened the door before he had a chance to come around to open it for her. She slid to the ground, pausing to grip the handle while she made sure she was steady on her feet. By the time Nate came around the truck, she'd shut the door and was moving toward the manor. He caught up with her and when she gripped the railing of the steps leading to the front door, he turned to look at her.

"You okay?" he asked.

"Just tired." Lily knew it was her stock answer to anyone querying her slowness, but it was never one hundred percent the truth.

He waited for her at the top of the steps and then opened the door to the foyer. Suddenly eager to be away from him and the reminder of all his gentlemanly gestures, Lily said, "Thanks again for the ride. I think I'm just going to go on up."

"Me, too. I would imagine the week ahead is going to be pretty busy." He paused for a second and then said, "I told Lance that I would be willing to move to the motel since you're home now. He said I should stay, but I want that to be up to you."

It would make things much easier if he were living someplace else. But she knew that it would be wrong to send him off just to make things easier on herself. He needed the security of the manor as much as she did. "It's fine by me if you stay here. So much better than the motel."

He slowly nodded. "By a long shot."

Lily had hoped he'd go to the kitchen to get a drink or something first so she could get up the stairs on her own. Instead, she was forced to push herself to climb the stairs as normally as possible. Once at the top, she said good night to him and headed into her room, closing the door firmly behind her.

She leaned against it and took a deep breath. Hurdle number one over. It hadn't been as bad as she had anticipated, but her traitorous heart wanted things it couldn't have. Hurdle number two was telling her family about her diagnosis and what it meant for her. That one would be hard, but she hoped that in sharing all the information she'd gathered over the past three years, they would be able to accept it the way she had.

తుళ

Nate stared at Lily's closed door. Seeing her again had

been harder than he had imagined it would be. He'd been so angry at her for ending their engagement and leaving so abruptly that he hadn't thought there was still love in his heart for her. He'd known there was still healing that needed to occur, but love? Seeing her at the concert tonight and then afterward sitting on the bench outside the church, he realized that his heart still felt so much for her. Too much. Crystal had sensed it, and now he knew that she was right.

But the Lily he'd just shared a ride home with was different. She'd calmed in the three years they'd been apart. She'd always liked to talk, which had worked well for them since he hadn't. And then she hadn't waited for him to come and help her from the truck. It was a poignant reminder that she no longer had that expectation of him. She was capable of taking care of herself and seemed to want him to know it.

He turned away from the sight of her closed door and headed for his room. Once inside he flopped back on the bed, staring up at the ceiling. What concerned him most were the differences in her physically. He knew her body—better than he likely should have—enough to know that something was different. Her slow, cautious movements were so unlike the Lily he'd been engaged to. He'd often called her *Lily-Belle*, his version of Tinker Bell, because of how she'd seemed to flutter around him.

There was no fluttering anymore. Just cautious, steady movements. He tried to tell himself it was just a maturing on her part, but he wondered if there was something more serious going on. She'd never given him a definite reason for ending their engagement. She had just said she didn't think it would work out for them, that they were too different. While Nate agreed that they were different, it hadn't been a problem in their relationship up to that point. How was it after almost seven years together, it suddenly became an issue?

He hoped that perhaps her presence here would give him a chance to gain the closure he needed in order to move on. Crystal's words were proof that he hadn't gotten to that point yet, but perhaps having her back in his life would give him a chance to see that things were really and truly over between them.

His heart clenched at the thought and with a groan, he rolled to his stomach. This was just the very last thing he needed right then. God had a lousy sense of timing if He thought that Nate could deal with Lily's return on top of everything else that had been dropped on him over the past few days. But he would do what he always did.

Chin up. Shoulders back. Tackle the issues head on.

ഏൽ

At Lily's request, her sisters and Will gathered at the manor the following afternoon. Because Jessa was still confined to bed, they were all up in the room with her.

"I know you all have wondered about my sudden departure after I ended my engagement with Nate." Lily shifted on the chair she'd chosen. Her stomach was in knots. She wanted to present this in such a way as to minimize their alarm or concern.

"We figured you didn't want to be around Nate after you ended things," Violet said. "But we didn't expect you to stay away for so long."

"I didn't either. I just needed some time to adjust."

"And you've adjusted now?" Laurel asked. After Lily had nodded, she continued, "But what have you adjusted to?"

Lily took a deep breath. "About nine months before I left, I had an issue with my left eye. I didn't mention it at the time, but I was really scared."

"Why didn't you tell me?" Jessa asked, an edge of hurt to her words.

"I didn't want to worry anyone. I thought it was nothing. It did seem to get better as time went on, and I convinced myself not to worry about it. Then about three months after the first problem, I had it again in the same eye along with other things. Some numbness and weakness in my legs. This time I went to the doctor. He immediately set me up for an eye exam which was then followed by an MRI. He knew what he was looking at but did the tests anyway."

"What was he looking at?" Will was leaned against the wall, arms crossed over his chest.

"MS. He was pretty sure it was MS because his wife had had similar symptoms before being diagnosed."

"Multiple sclerosis?" Cami spoke for the first time. "You have MS? You faced that diagnosis on your own?"

Lily clenched her hands in her lap and looked down. "You all had so much else going on in your lives, I didn't want to burden you. I wasn't willing to accept the diagnosis right away either. I figured if you guys knew, you'd force me to deal with it head on. And while I know now that would have been the smart thing, it wasn't what I felt I needed then."

Will came close and sank onto one knee next to her, his hand covering hers. "Does Nate know?"

Lily shook her head. "I couldn't tell him. There were things I needed to do, and I knew he couldn't do them with me. And then there was his mother."

"His mother?" Will prompted.

Lily looked up into her brother's concerned eyes. "His dad spent a lot of time caring for his mom before she died. I didn't want to burden Nate with the same fate. Even though I am still basically okay now, there will come a time when I will require more help. I didn't want him to become my care-giver, but I knew that he would do it without complaint because of the type of man he is. I just didn't want that to happen. I don't want to be a burden to anyone."

There was silence for a long moment then Laurel said, "You would never be a burden to us, Lily Grace. You should know that by now. We're family, and we're there for each other. Good, bad and ugly."

"Well, this has certainly got the bad and ugly," Lily said with a small smile.

"But the good is that you're back home." Violet came to kneel next to Will. She covered both their hands with hers and looked intently at Lily. "And we're going to get through this as a family. You need to explain to us all about the disease and tell us what we need to do to make it easier for you."

Tears sprang to Lily's eyes but with her hands trapped, they spilled unchecked down her cheeks. "Thank you. These past couple of years—once I accepted the diagnosis—have given me a chance to become reacquainted with my body and to discover what my new normal is."

"How difficult has it been for you?" Jessa asked.

Will and Violet stood and moved aside so Lily could see Jessa. Lily got up and approached the bed, taking Jessa's hand when she held it out. As she sank down beside her oldest sister, she could see the worry on her face.

"It was very hard at first. I was angry. Couldn't figure out why it happened to me." Lily intertwined her fingers. "One of the reasons I went to London was that I had planned to travel at some point years down the road. I figured there would come a day when Nate and I could travel around the world together. When I realized what being diagnosed with MS meant in the long run, I was determined to get my traveling in while I still could."

"Were you able to do that?"

"Yes, but at a cost to myself. By not seeking medical help right away, I suffered more than I should have. But I wised up and once I found a good doctor and a support group, I was able to learn how to cope with it while still not letting it take over my life completely."

Cami settled on the bed on the other side of Jessa. "What made you come home now?"

"It was time. I'd seen what I needed to of Europe. I had a better handle on the disease and how to live with it. But most of all, I just missed you all. I needed to be home."

"I expect you to give a full run-down on what you need from us and how we can help you with this," Jessa said, a determined look on her face. "Well, I won't be much help at the moment, but I want to be informed."

Lily smiled at Jessa, the sister who had stepped up to care for her when Gran had begun to slip away from the family. "I will answer all your questions and will give you any information you want."

"Day to day, what is your biggest challenge?" Jessa asked.

"I find that if I get enough sleep and eat a decent diet, my body reacts better. If I get overtired, my emotions go out of whack and my body is slow to respond. My legs cause me the most problems. They go numb at times, but more often than that, they get weak, which makes walking a challenge sometimes. But attacks can happen without warning and then I just have to deal with the symptoms as they manifest themselves. So far I've had two really bad attacks, but both times I was able to recover completely because of medicine and therapy. That might not always be the case in the years to come."

"What caused it?" It didn't surprise Lily that Jessa was the one with the most questions. She had always been the one to approach any problem armed with as much info as possible.

Lily shrugged. "There really is no definite cause. They have theories, but there is nothing they can pinpoint that would have caused mine. The thing about this disease is that it is unpredictable. I could go years without another attack, or I could have one tomorrow. It could be twenty years before things began to progress more rapidly or it could be next year. I just have to take it day by day."

Violet came up to her and hugged her tightly. "Well, no more running away. We're here to help you."

Even though they had more questions, Lily breathed a sigh of relief. The worst was over. She'd worried about their reactions, particularly Jessa's, but apparently it had been for nothing. No doubt they still didn't understand completely why she'd chosen to leave when she'd been given the news.

Though she regretted the hurt she'd caused her family, Lily knew that the time away had been exactly what she'd needed. During that initial period, she'd been able to feel the raw emotions that had filled her as a result of the diagnosis. She hadn't had to hide them from anyone. She hadn't had anyone breathing down her neck telling her what to do and not to do. She'd run from the diagnosis until it had brought her—quite literally—to her knees.

Once she'd come face to face with it, the moment of truth had woken her up and since that point, she had worked hard to educate herself and get good medical care while in Europe. Lily was eternally grateful for the inheritance that had allowed her to seek out the care she'd needed for the duration of her time there. Most who faced the diagnosis didn't have the resources she had because of her family's wealth. Now back home, she would once again seek out the best care she could. She was not in denial about what she needed or what was to come, but she also didn't want it to overwhelm her life.

She still hadn't decided what—if anything—to tell Nate. It wouldn't make any difference in their relationship now. The bottom line would always remain the same, she couldn't—and wouldn't—saddle him with her care in later years.

"I've got to head back to the office," Will said.

Lily stood up to give him a hug. "Thank you for coming out on such short notice."

Will looked down at her. "I wish it were for a different reason, but I'm glad you've told us now. Is it okay if I share this with Amy?"

"Certainly. I expected each of you would share it with your spouses or significant others."

Will's expression tensed. "Do you plan to tell Nate?"

❧ Chapter Five ❧

LILY glanced around at her siblings, each with expectant expressions on their faces. "No. I mean, I'm not trying to keep it a secret. But I'm not going to have a conversation with him about it. Our relationship is over, and from what I've heard, he's moved on."

"He brought you home last night," Will pointed out.

"Yes. And I appreciated that, but there was no talk of taking up where we left off."

"I still think you should tell him. He's probably wondered about you leaving, just like we have."

Lily crossed her arms. "I'll think about it. Right now, it seems like maybe he has a lot on his plate already. Do you really think he needs to deal with all of this from me?"

Will tilted his head. "I suppose not, but you coming back is probably giving him something to deal with if he never really had closure before. Sorry, just coming from a guy's perspective. I'd want to know."

"I'll think about it," Lily said. "If you feel he should know about the MS, you're welcome to tell him. I just don't want to dredge up all the old relationship stuff which is inevitable if I sit down to talk to him about it."

"It might be easier coming from me," Will admitted. "If you're sure you're okay with that."

Lily shrugged. "If you think it would be best that he know then hearing it from you is probably better than me."

"He's a good guy who's had a bad turn of events in the past few years. I feel for the guy."

"You don't have to tell me he's a good guy," Lily reminded him. "I was with him for seven years. I didn't leave him because he was a bad guy. I left him because I felt he deserved better."

Will looked like he was going to say something more, but Cami laid her hand on his arm. "Will, I know you see things in the light of your relationship with Amy, but Lily might have a different path to take."

Lily watched as Will frowned at Cami but then he nodded. He let out a long sigh. "Fine. No more talking about Nate."

"Thank you," Lily said. "I appreciate you wanting to look out for him—he probably needs that more than ever—but getting involved with me again is not in his best interests."

Will gave her another quick hug before leaving the room. Once he was gone, there was silence in the room. Lily looked around. "Do you guys think he's right?"

"Well, until I ended up on bed rest, I would have agreed with him. But after being confined here and having to have people wait on me hand and foot, I understand what it's like to feel as if you're a burden. Lance never complains, but I know that it's added to his stress to have to deal with my needs on top of all his other responsibilities." Jessa ran a hand over her burgeoning stomach. "I will be glad to get back to being able to pull my own weight. So I do understand why you wouldn't want to place that kind of responsibility on Nate, even if it is years from now."

"But Jessa, you know Lance does what he does for you out

of love and would never view it as a burden," Laurel said. "None of us who have helped out these past several weeks have viewed it that way. And maybe Nate wouldn't view it that way either because he loves Lily."

"Loved." Her heart clenched as she corrected her sister.

Laurel glanced at her and shrugged. "Back when you first got the news he loved you. He didn't get to have a say."

"Do you really think—knowing Nate and the type of guy he is—that he would have agreed to end things because of my diagnosis? Would he have stayed with me out of a sense of obligation since we were already engaged, or would he have stayed with me out of love? I would never have known for sure, and I couldn't live with that."

"I think we're coming at this from many different perspectives," Jessa said. "In the end, it is Lily's decision because it's her life. She is the one that has to live with this disease and all that encompasses. I don't know what I would have done in her position. None of us do."

"You're right," Violet agreed. She came to where Lily stood and wrapped her arms around her. "Just know that we love you and are here for you for the long haul. Never hesitate to tell us what you need."

Laurel joined the embrace followed by Cami. Lily felt tears prick her eyes once again, but blinked to keep them at bay. Because of the six to ten year age gap between her and them, at one time she had felt on the outside of things when it came to her sisters. However, after these past few years on her own, Lily knew she had matured, and now the age difference didn't seem as significant. She was truly thankful for their presence in her life.

"Hey, no fair," Jessa protested. "I can't get in on the group hug."

Laughing, the four women joined Jessa on the bed to include her in another embrace. It was wonderful to have such a normal sisterly moment after the heaviness of her revelation. Lily knew, more than ever, that her decision to come home had been the right one.

♋♋

Nate stalked through the garage. The scent of burnt wood still lingered in the air, but hopefully after a couple of days of having the garage open it would dissipate. The majority of the damage had been done to the back corner of the building which was where his office was. For the time being, he'd have to do his paperwork elsewhere.

The sounds of the mechanics at work soothed him somewhat. At least it was the sound of what normal had been before everything had fallen to pieces. He was glad that the fire marshal had cleared him to reopen the garage sooner than expected provided they steered clear of the corner of the building that had been damaged. That wasn't an issue since the guys rarely went to his office. In fact, he avoided his office if at all possible as well.

"Everything okay?"

Nate turned to see the manager of the garage approaching him. "Hey, Don. Glad to see you guys all here this morning."

"Yep. We're glad to be able to get back to work. Know it can't be easy for the guys in Sanford. You gonna re-open there?"

"Not anytime soon. The garage there is in the same state as my house here. It will have to be ripped right down and rebuilt. I still have to work with the insurance to see what their final settlement will be. Not something I'm looking forward to, but in the meantime the guys in Sanford will have to find other jobs, I think."

"That's a shame. Especially for Marty. Really like that guy."

"Me, too." Nate rubbed a hand over his head. "I would consider bringing him on here, but there's not enough work. Plus I doubt he wants to drive this far for a job."

"Yeah, not likely any of these guys are going to quit on

you. They all like you too much."

Nate gave Don a weary smile. "I'm grateful for that."

"They catch the guy yet? The one who did this?"

"Nope. Last I heard they had rounded up some of his buddies, but no one was talking."

One of the mechanics called for Don, and after he had excused himself, Nate continued on to his office. He wanted to take a peek, just to see how much damage there was. He supposed he should be thankful that early last week he'd accepted Don's offer to have his teenage daughter come in to scan all his un-entered invoices into his computer. All of that was now available to him through his online backup. He needed to do a deposit as well to get all the money into the bank and then pay some bills. Life had to go on. Thankfully Lance had offered him the use of the library at the manor until he was able to get back into his office at the garage.

Nate collected the cash and checks from the fireproof safe that had preserved them. After he'd gathered what he needed, he headed back out into the garage area. He spotted Don standing with one of the mechanics and interrupted them briefly to let him know that he would be available by phone if anything came up that needed his attention.

Back at the manor, he carried the file box inside.

"Hey, Nate," Amy greeted him with a smile. "How're things going at the garage?"

"As well as can be expected. Very thankful that it is still functional."

"It's horrible how much damage fire can do. My mom said the other day they're just finally getting around to clearing out the damaged building at my old school."

"Yeah, I'm not sure when I'll be able to tackle the mess in Sanford." He lifted the box. "Lance told me I could make use of the library here since my office was damaged in the fire."

"Sure, it's just through there." Amy motioned with her hand. "We're having a bit of a late lunch today. Can I make you a sandwich?"

"I hate to be a bother," Nate said, though food sounded very appealing since he hadn't had breakfast that morning.

Amy laughed. "It's no bother to make another sandwich. Ham okay?"

"Yep. I'm not fussy."

"I'll bring it to you when it's ready."

Nate thanked her then headed for the library. He put the box on the desk before heading up to his room to grab his laptop which had been spared in the fire since he'd had it with him in Sanford. He glanced toward Lily's room, not surprised to see the door was closed. It was possible she wasn't even in the manor right then. Not that it mattered to him.

Or at least that's what he kept telling himself.

Back in the library, he settled down at the desk and let out a long sigh before opening his laptop. This was absolutely the part of the job he hated the most. He and his dad had slowly been turning over the paperwork side of things to Lily. She'd taken some courses on bookkeeping at the college in order to help them out. It had pleased Nate to have Lily working alongside him in the business that would one day have been theirs. But then she'd just up and left...

Nate stared at the screen of the laptop, trying to pull his thoughts back from that path. He'd been on the verge of hiring a bookkeeper to help him out, but that would have to be put on hold. For now, he'd have to keep doing it himself and hope his accountant could sort it all out come tax time.

With a couple of clicks of the mouse, he pulled up the page that showed his uploaded files. He breathed a sigh of relief when he saw that the files were all there. He'd been pretty sure they would be, but he had needed to see it for himself.

Nate had been working for about twenty minutes, fighting frustration at having to flip back and forth between screens to enter the data into his accounting program, when he heard movement at the door of the library. He glanced up, surprised to see it wasn't Amy as he'd expected, but Lily.

"Hey, Nate." She stepped into the library, a tray balanced somewhat awkwardly on her forearms as her hands gripped the outside edge, pressing it against her torso. "Amy asked me to bring you some lunch. Is this a good time?"

Nate pushed back from the desk and stood. "When it comes to bookwork, I'm always happy for a break." He took the tray from her and set it on the desk. "I'm still trying to decide if I'm happy or not that most of my paperwork survived the fire."

Lily tilted her head, her deep auburn hair sliding like a wave of silk over her shoulder. "Can I help you? I know it's been awhile, but I think I could probably figure it out."

Nate wanted to accept her offer, but he wasn't sure it would be a good idea. "Thanks, but I think it's best if I just stick to it."

Lily took a step back, her hands clenched at her waist. She nodded before turning on her heel and leaving the library.

Why did he feel guilty for turning her down? She was the one who'd walked away. Did she really think they could have a half relationship? Picking up some parts of their past but leaving other parts alone? He didn't think he was strong enough to do that right then. It hurt to think she had gotten to that point. He realized each time he saw her that he hadn't. And there was no way he would ever get there if he allowed himself to work shoulder to shoulder with her.

Rounding the desk, Nate sank back down into the chair. He picked up half the sandwich and bit into it, no longer hungry but knowing he needed some sort of sustenance. Unfortunately, though he finished the sandwich, he just couldn't focus on what was on the screen. His thoughts kept going to Lily and her offer. Really, what could it hurt? They were both adults, and God knew he really could use the help.

Not giving himself the opportunity to change his mind, Nate pushed back from the desk and walked from the room. Following the scent of baked goods, he went first to the kitchen where he found Amy and Cami making cookies. There were several racks cooling on the counter. He glanced around, thinking Lily might be with them.

"Smells good," Nate said when they looked in his direction.

"Want some?" Amy set the sheet she held onto the counter. "Nothing like fresh baked oatmeal chocolate chip cookies."

"Thanks. Maybe later. Right now, I need to talk to Lily. Is she around?"

Nate didn't miss the glance exchanged by the two women.

Cami began to move cookies from the rack to a plastic container. "She's upstairs in her room."

"Thank you," Nate said, though he felt the information was given rather grudgingly.

It was almost like they thought he was going to hurt her or something. Did they forget that she was the one who had broken up with *him*? He climbed the stairs, determined to keep this professional. Once at her closed door, he rapped lightly.

Shoving his hands into his pockets, he waited for her answer. It took longer than he had thought it would before the door opened. Her hair looked a bit rumpled as if she'd been sleeping.

Lily's eyes widened when she saw him.

He shifted his weight from one foot to the other. "I was thinking about your offer. The one about helping with the bookkeeping."

Lily leaned against the edge of the door. "You want me to help you?"

"If the offer still stands."

The way she stared at him, her face expressionless, unnerved Nate. At one time he had been able to read her easily, but as she looked at him with those big green eyes, he had no idea what was going through her mind. "It does." She tilted her head. "Do you need my help now?"

"If it's convenient for you."

"Sure. I'll be down in a couple of minutes."

"Thanks." Nate waited until she'd shut the door again before heading back downstairs. He swung by the kitchen to grab a few cookies.

"Did you get to talk to her?" Cami asked as she placed the cookies on a plate for him.

"Yes. She offered to help me with the bookkeeping for the garage. It's what she used to do...before. I initially turned her down because...well, history and everything, but I really do need help. I'm dealing with so much that if I can get help with that part, it would be great."

"Well, here are some cookies to help ease the process." Cami handed him the plate.

"Ready to get to work?" Lily asked as she walked into the kitchen.

Nate noticed she'd pulled her hair back into a ponytail and now wore a pair of glasses. The glasses took him by surprise because she never used them before. Just one more change that unsettled him. "Yep. No time like the present."

Carrying the plate of cookies, Nate followed Lily to the library. She settled into the chair he'd vacated earlier and leaned forward, bracing her forearms on the desk. As she stared at the screen, he tried to explain what he'd been doing. He leaned close to point to the screen and got a whiff of something light and floral. It was hard to keep his thoughts on the business at hand when all he could think about was how he'd loved to run his fingers through her hair. It had been like fragrant silk, smooth and soft in his hands.

Pulling his thoughts back to the laptop, Nate said, "The biggest pain about trying to do this is having to flip back and forth from the pdf file to the accounting program. If they could just be side by side, it would make things a lot easier, but the screen just isn't big enough."

"You need a second monitor," Lily said.

Nate straightened. "I can hook up a second monitor to my laptop?"

"Pretty sure." Lily turned the laptop around to look at the back of it. "Yep. You can hook it up here."

"Well, then I'm going to go get one." Nate knew he couldn't afford to be buying stuff willy-nilly, but right then it seemed important that he be able to get the paperwork done. With the desktop computer ruined from water and smoke damage, he was going to have to use the laptop for the time being.

Lily looked up at him. "Like you said, it would be easier to be able to view both screens at the same time. Dual monitors are the best way to do that."

"Can I get something like that at Walmart?"

A small smile played around the corners of her mouth. "Yes. They do carry monitors."

"Is there a brand I should buy? And a certain size?"

She paused then said, "Do you want me to come with you?"

Not allowing himself to consider another option, Nate nodded. "You've always been a bit more up on the computer side of things than I have."

"You use computers at the garage," she pointed out.

"Yeah, but they're connected to something I *do* understand. Cars."

"Let me get my purse." Lily slowly stood up. She braced her hand for a second on the desk then moved around him toward the door. "I'll be right back."

Nate grabbed a couple of the cookies and took a bite of one as he dug his keys out of his pocket. He was kind of surprised that she'd suggested going with him. Maybe this was her attempt to get their relationship to a "just friends" place. Being with her made it difficult to get to that point since his heart really wasn't interested in friendship.

This time Nate steered clear of the kitchen while he waited for Lily. As he stood in the hallway eating the second cookie he'd taken, he heard Amy and Cami talking.

"Did Will tell you if he was going to talk to Nate?" Cami asked. "He seemed pretty determined that Nate should know."

"He did mention it before he left for the office. I'm not sure that's the right decision. I think Lily should be the one to decide to share anything with Nate."

"I guess it must be something about guys sticking together. I feel the same way you do."

Nate scowled. What were they talking about? Was there some big secret Lily hadn't told him? He heard movement and glanced up to see Lily making her way down the stairs. Once again, she moved more slowly than he remembered. Of course, in the past, she'd always been excited to see him. She'd practically flown down the stairs to meet him when he'd come to pick her up. There was no rush for her to join him now.

The thought caused an ache in his heart. More than anything he wanted back what they'd once had. They'd been together for almost seven years. No one else had ever known him as well as she had. Clearly he had failed to achieve anything similar with Crystal, given what she'd said. He knew he'd held back part of himself from her. After all, he had no guarantee that she wouldn't leave him like Lily had. And of course there was the fact that he just hadn't felt that closeness with her. Top it off with all the responsibility that had landed solely on his shoulders with his dad's death, and it hadn't been an ideal set of circumstances in which to nurture a relationship.

"Ready to go?" Lily asked as she stepped toward him, her purse strap slung over her shoulder.

"If you are." At her nod, he headed for the front door and held it open for her. He did the same with the door of his truck. Though she made no comment, he got the feeling she'd rather he didn't do those things for her.

Too bad.

He assumed that she saw them spending time together as a way to show him they could be friends. From his perspective, however, he saw it as an opportunity to remind her of how good they were together.

"So how was Europe?" Nate asked as he guided the truck down the driveway to the road leading to Collingsworth.

"Beautiful. I was able to cross off all the places on my 'must see' list."

"I should hope so, considering you were over there for almost three years." Silence hung heavy between them. "Uh, what was your favorite place to visit?"

She didn't respond right away, and Nate figured he'd made her mad with his comment, but then she said, "It's really hard to choose just one place. Many of them were favorites for different reasons. But of course I enjoyed Paris. And visiting Scotland was a wonderful experience. But probably the chalet in Switzerland was my all-time favorite."

"I'm glad you enjoyed your time there," Nate said, though he really wanted to ask her if it had been worth it. Had it been worth losing their relationship over?

"It's good to be home though. It was time."

Nate sensed there was more. He was still in tuned enough to her to know that there was more to the story than what she was sharing. Was it the secret her sisters had been referring to earlier?

As they pulled into the Walmart parking lot, he let the conversation lapse. He found a spot near the entrance and parked. Once again, Lily got out of the truck before he had the opportunity to open her door for her. He knew he had to accept the new normal in dealing with her, but Nate didn't think he'd ever like it.

❧ Chapter Six ❧

LILY walked beside Nate through the automatic doors of the store. He grabbed a cart and together they made their way to the electronics section. Though she'd agreed to do this as a favor, she was really hoping she could prove to him—and herself—that friendship was possible. Collingsworth wasn't that big of a town, they were going to run into each other at least once a week at church if nowhere else. And since he was staying at the manor for the foreseeable future, it was even more important that they get past any awkwardness as soon as possible.

The unfortunate thing was, the more she was around him, the more she remembered how they were together. It was hard to be with someone for seven years and not know them intimately. Just walking into the store beside him brought on a barrage of memories. They had done it countless times before.

"So which one do you think I should get?" Nate's voice drew her from her memories, and she turned her focus to the shelf of monitors.

"Well, you don't want a super big one. I think that would

be a little impractical." She pointed to one that fell in the middle, size-wise. "Maybe that one would work."

She heard Nate mutter something as he stared at the monitor she'd indicated.

"What's that?" She could see frustration on his face as he glanced at her. "What's wrong?"

He scowled. "I must be the only man on the planet who needs a woman to show him about computers."

Lily laughed. "Oh, I doubt that's true. It just so happens that your talents lie in another area, and I happen to like electronic gadgets."

"Still. It's a little bit of a jab to the ego."

"Well, I won't tell anyone," Lily said.

Nate looked her way again then his gaze went past her. His expression changed and with a quick glance at her, he said, "I'll be right back."

She slowly turned as he walked past her, following his movements. He approached a woman who stood in the aisle just outside the electronics department. The woman had a mass of dark brown curls and came to a little above his shoulder, her figure curvy. Nate reached out and touched the woman's arm. The woman's gaze moved briefly in Lily's direction, but they were too far away for Lily to be able to read her expression. Was this Crystal?

Not wanting to intrude on a private moment, Lily turned back to face the monitors. Crossing her arms over her waist, she tried to quell the trembling that had taken over her stomach. She had no right to be jealous. But she was. Jealous of this woman whose health wouldn't lead to a life of dependency down the road. Jealous that she could be a helpmate to Nate rather than a burden. Jealous that she could have the life Lily had once dreamed about. No matter how much she'd come to accept her illness while in London, it was clear she hadn't truly let Nate go. She took a deep breath in and let it out.

In. Out.

Before he returned, she needed to be in control of her emotions. Her emotional extremes were so much closer to the surface than they'd once been, but she couldn't let Nate see her this way.

In. Out.

She heard footsteps approach and assumed they were Nate's. Lowering her arms, she bent her head as if reading the specs on the monitor.

"So, is this the one you think I should get?"

Lily glanced at him, glad he wasn't going to broach the subject of the woman. "Yes. I think it will work well."

Nate found a boxed monitor that matched the one on display and placed it in the cart. "Do you need anything else while we're here?"

"No. I'm good." There *were* actually a few things that she wouldn't have minded picking up, but at that point, all Lily wanted was to get back to the manor. She would see if Amy or Cami were coming in sometime in the next couple of days and hitch a ride.

An awkward silence stretched between them as they approached the cash registers at the front of the store. Aware that the likelihood of running into someone that knew her and/or Nate, Lily told him she'd wait on the other side of the registers for him.

Keeping her head bent, she flipped through screens on her phone while she waited.

"Lily?"

She looked up at the sound of her name and saw the woman Nate had been talking to earlier. "Yes?"

"Hi. My name is Crystal." She stuck out her hand.

Lily shook it, a bit unsure of how to respond. She glanced toward the registers and saw Nate watching them, his brows drawn together.

"I just wanted to meet you. I know what you mean to Nate, though he never spoke of you during our time together."

"You and Nate are dating?" Lily hoped there was no sign on her face of how the thought bothered her.

"No." The woman tilted her head to the side. "We were, but when I heard you were back in town, I broke it off."

Lily frowned. "Why did you do that? I'm not back to rekindle things with Nate."

"Maybe not, but I'd always told myself that if you came back before certain things had happened in my relationship with him that I would break things off." Crystal's smile had an edge of sadness to it. "I always thought that in time, he'd come to feel about me like I did about him. That didn't happen."

Lily wasn't sure what to say to this woman. "I'm...sorry?"

"Don't be. If it had been meant to be, we would have been in a different place by now. He's a wonderful man." Another sad smile. "Maybe if it's not meant to be with you either, he can at least gain some closure by you coming back."

"I hope so. I'm not the right woman for him." Lily's heart clenched as she said the words.

"I think he'd disagree with you."

"I'm sorry it didn't work out for you." Though she knew her heart was still tangled up with Nate, she really did hope he could find happiness with someone else. It might be her destiny to be on her own, but it didn't have to be Nate's.

The woman shrugged. "I'm going to assume God has someone else out there for me." She reached out and touched Lily's arm. "Anyway, I just wanted to meet you. I figured you must be someone pretty special to still hold his heart the way you do."

As the woman turned and walked away, Lily stared after her. The conversation did nothing to strengthen her resolve to keep her relationship with Nate on a strictly friendship level. She had to keep reminding herself that the decision she'd made was for the benefit of both of them. Given the type of man he was, Lily knew he would never have agreed to end things once he learned of her diagnosis. He would have stuck by her whether he wanted to or not. She just couldn't have borne the weight of that.

"Ready?"

She looked over to see that he had joined her. When she nodded, he began to push the cart toward the exit of the store. Though he said nothing, she could feel the questions he had about her conversation with Crystal. Unfortunately, there was no way she could share it with him without having to delve into their past.

Once at the truck, he opened her door for her and closed it once she was settled. Lily leaned her head back against the seat. She heard him open and close the back door on the driver's side before sliding behind the wheel.

"Here."

Lily looked over and saw him holding out a chocolate bar. Chocolate with almonds. Her favorite. She met his gaze briefly before reaching out to take the bar from his hand. Her fingertips brushed across his palm. "You didn't have to do that."

"I know. Consider it a thank you for helping me out with this monitor."

Clutching the chocolate bar in her hand, Lily said, "You're welcome."

"Aren't you going to eat it now?" he asked as he backed out of the parking spot.

"I'm not hungry at the moment." That wasn't the real reason though. In the past when he'd bought her a chocolate bar, she'd always shared with him. It wasn't that she didn't want to share, it was just that it would bring an intimacy to the moment that she couldn't handle right then. "I'll save it for when I need a break from your bookkeeping."

"Well, I'm sure you'll need that sooner rather than later."

They drove in silence once again, but as they headed north out of Collingsworth, Nate said, "Want to share what you and Crystal were talking about?"

"No. That's going to have to stay between her and me." Lily slipped the chocolate bar into her purse. "She seems like a nice woman."

"She is."

And that was the last of their conversation for the duration of the trip.

"Are there directions on how to set this up?" Nate asked as he freed the monitor from its cardboard and Styrofoam prison once they were back in the library.

"I don't need them." Lily undid the cords that were bound by a plastic zip tie. "I've done this a time or two before."

Lily was glad to have something to focus on after the awkward ride home. This was definitely not working out how she'd planned. So far, it had all backfired on her. Instead of helping to build a friendship with Nate, being around him like this was just reminding her of how much she'd missed having him in her life.

Nate snapped the monitor into its base then took the ends of the cords Lily handed him.

"There should be a spot to plug those in on the back of the monitor." She took the other ends and plugged one into the laptop and one into the power bar under the desk. After the other monitor had turned on, she sat down in the chair and began to go through the steps of setting it up as a second monitor for the laptop.

She was acutely aware of Nate's presence behind her but managed to keep her attention on the task at hand. Once the monitor functioned the way she wanted, she showed him how it would work.

"That's perfect," he said. "Thank you for your help with this."

"You're welcome. And now I'll get to work inputting the invoices into your system."

Nate bent over her shoulder, his chest brushing against her arm. He touched a file on the screen, and as it popped open, he said, "This is where I had Don's daughter scan all the invoices. Do you need me to go through them with you?"

Lily tried to keep herself focused on Nate's words, not his nearness or the familiar scent of his cologne. "Not unless you've changed things significantly over the past few years."

"No." She felt him straighten. "Everything is the same."

Lily looked at him as he moved to the side of the desk. "You don't need to hang around here while I do this. If I have any questions, I'll give you a call or save it for later."

His eyes narrowed briefly. "Trying to get rid of me?"

"There's no sense in both of us being tied up here when it only takes one to do this. I'm sure there are other more important things that could use your attention."

Nate stared at her, his face expressionless. "Yes, you're probably right." He turned away from her and headed for the door.

"Is your number still the same?" Lily called after him.

He stopped then swung back around. "Yes. It, too, is still the same."

Lily stared at the empty doorway once he'd left. There had been an undercurrent of...something...emanating from him. Anger? That's what it had felt like. Though she knew Nate could get as angry as the next guy, that anger had never been directed toward her. Whatever he'd been feeling in that moment had definitely been flowing her way.

Pushing aside her thoughts, Lily stood for a moment and slowly stretched her back and legs. If she was going to be sitting for a while, she needed to make sure she took breaks to keep from getting too sore. Then it was down to work on the mess that was Nate's bookkeeping.

❧☙

Nate stomped on the accelerator of his truck when he got on the highway. The big vehicle surged up to the speed limit in no time flat. He fought the urge to edge it up, but the last thing he wanted was to have to rely on the sheriff's understanding and goodwill to avoid a speeding ticket. Keeping an eye on the speedometer, he felt relief slowly overtake the frustration as he put distance between himself and the manor.

Try as he might, Nate just couldn't seem to keep his life from spinning even more out of control than it already had. Ever since that night almost three years ago, nothing had gone right.

"I'm sorry, Nate. I just don't think it's going to work for us." Though Lily's voice was determined, all Nate saw on her face was tension and weariness.

Pain engulfed his heart and took his breath away. Fighting past the agony that was slowly spreading through his body, Nate asked, "How can it suddenly not work for us? It's been working fine for almost seven years. What's changed?"

"Me." Lily laid a hand over her heart.

"Is there someone else?" He had to force the words out.

Her eyes widened as she shook her head. "No, please don't think that. This is just about me. I need to..." Her words trailed off as her brow furrowed. "I need to do more than just hang around Collingsworth. I want...more. To travel. See the world."

Nate's eyes closed briefly as he recalled the conversation he'd had with her several months back about traveling. When she'd mentioned taking a trip somewhere, he'd immediately shot it down. After all, he had responsibilities there with his dad and the business. "If I said I'd be willing to take a trip with you every few months would that change things?"

Her mouth tightened. "You and I both know that would never happen. You have responsibilities here. And you're not the type of man to shirk those."

Nate's shoulders slumped. She was right. His priority would always be his father and the business. As he stared at Lily standing in front of him, her hair glinting in the sunlight, he knew that he hadn't even given her the priority he should have. Maybe this was just what he deserved. "Is there anything I can say or do that will make you change your mind about us?"

Lily shook her head. "I think this is for the best. You need someone who is content to stay here in Collingsworth. That's not me."

"But do we have to break up? Can't you just travel and then come back?"

Again she shook her head. "That's not fair to you or to me." She reached up and touched the outside edge of her eye, almost as if it were paining her. "This really is what is best for both of us."

It hurt to think that this felt right to her, because it certainly didn't feel that way to him. He'd always assumed she'd be there for him forever. He'd just taken that for granted. He'd hoped that they would have a relationship similar to the one his parents had. Before his mom had gotten sick.

After that, his parents' relationship had changed. Though his dad had done his best to care for her, his mom had struggled with the burden she'd placed on her husband and son. That meant there had been days when she was angry. The next day she'd be depressed. The only good day was the one where she felt she was able to do things on her own. But she'd always paid for it the day after, which would then lead to more angry and depressed days.

But even with that, Nate had been willing to pledge to be with Lily forever. He just couldn't imagine his future without her in it.

Lily slid the ring off her finger and held it out to him. "I'm sorry."

She really did seem to be sorry. Her beautiful green eyes were liquid with unshed tears. If it hurt her this much, too, how could it be the right thing?

He didn't want the ring. Refused to take it. A tear spilled down her cheek as she took a step toward him. She placed her hand on the side of his face and leaned forward to touch her lips to his briefly. He wanted to grab her and hold on. To keep her lips pressed to his. He was going to have to go the rest of his life without ever feeling her in his arms again. Without ever looking into her eyes to see them sparkling with love for him.

She took his hand, turned it palm up and placed the ring there. Using both her hands, she closed his fingers around the ring and held on for just a second before letting go and stepping back. "Take care of yourself, Nate."

Pain shredding his heart, Nate watched as she walked away from him. Don't go! he wanted to shout after her, but he knew there was no use. When Lily made up her mind, there was no changing it. Except for him. At one time, he'd thought she'd decided to be with him. Something had changed her mind. And as he watched her determinedly walk out of his life, Nate knew he had better not hold his breath that she'd change her mind once more.

Angry with himself for allowing his mind to take that trip down memory lane, Nate swung the truck to a stop in his parking spot next to the garage. He sat behind the wheel for a few minutes trying to regain his composure. His gaze drifted to the blackened structure next to the garage that had once been his home. Right now, his heart felt a bit like it had been wrecked in the same way.

But he refused to focus on that right now either. His past with Lily had to be off limits. There was too much that needed his attention in the present to allow things from the past to keep taking up his time and emotions. And there was no sense in beating on a door that led nowhere. He should have accepted that years ago, but instead he'd allowed himself to harbor hope in his heart that one day Lily would come back.

Well, she had returned. Just not to him.

๑ Chapter Seven ๑

READY for a break?"

Lily looked up to see Cami standing on the other side of the desk. She slid her glasses off, fighting the urge to rub her eyes. "What time is it?"

"Almost three. You've been at it for about an hour and a half. I would think a break would do you good."

Lily nodded. "It would. I had planned to take regular breaks, but I guess I kind of got caught up in this."

"C'mon," Cami said with a wave of her hand. "Let's go outside for a bit. It's not too hot today."

"Been doing a little research?" Lily asked as she stood up. She pressed her hands against the small of her back and stretched.

"You bet. The only way to be able to help you is to understand what you're dealing with."

Lily rounded the desk and joined Cami as they left the library. "Seems awful quiet. Where are the kids?"

"Josh and Amy took them all off to a park somewhere

once they were done with lunch. I think Laurel and Violet went, too."

"You didn't want to go?"

"Not really. I'm never one to turn down a little peace and quiet." Cami smiled. "Plus, we thought someone should be here for you and Jessa."

Lily sighed. "I'm not an invalid. Yet, anyway. I can take care of myself."

"I know, but we're still getting used to that. You're going to have to cut us a little slack."

"I'll try. I know I have a couple years' head start on dealing with this. And even that doesn't seem to matter sometimes. Just when you think you've got it figured out, something new pops up. The number one thing I've learned from my own research and living with MS myself is that it's not the same for everyone. My journey with MS will be completely different from someone else's. It's unpredictable, which makes it that much more challenging." Lily lifted her face to the breeze as they stepped out onto the porch. She had missed this while living in London. The silence was broken only by the rustle of the leaves and other sounds of nature.

She followed Cami down the steps to the lawn chairs. With a contented sigh, she sank down onto one of the chaise lounges and stretched her legs out.

"What I read also said stress aggravates things for you." Cami settled down on the chair beside her. "Is being around Nate a stress for you? Will it make things harder?"

"I didn't think it would, but now I'm not so sure. Being away from here meant being away from reminders. Memories are much harder to fight when the trigger is right in front of you."

"Should I talk to Lance about asking him to move?"

Lily jerked her head around to stare at Cami. "No. He's going through so much already, I wouldn't dream of adding to that. I think this is where he needs to be. I'll be fine. Just have to get over the initial rush of memories. I'm hoping that being around him more will help us get to that point of friendship."

"Good luck with that," Cami said. "From what I've seen, I don't think friendship is what Nate wants."

"Well, it's all he's going to get." Lily stared out over the back yard, her gaze going to the chapel set back in the corner of the trees. At one time, she'd dreamed of her and Nate's wedding taking place there. It had all been planned out in her mind. They just hadn't made it to the altar. No one knew that she'd actually found her perfect dream dress and had ordered it just months before she'd received the diagnosis and everything changed. It was in storage at the bridal shop in Collingsworth. She had paid for them to store it until her return. She would need to go get it soon. Or maybe see if they could sell it for her, because there was no reason to hang onto it any longer.

"Earth to Lily."

Lily glanced at Cami. "Sorry."

"No problem. Anything you want to talk about?"

"No. You'll have to forgive me if I lapse into silence. I've spent a lot of time alone with my own thoughts over the past couple of years."

Cami frowned. "Did you not make friends where you lived?"

Lily thought back to the people who had lived in the other flats in the building where she'd rented. She'd known them all and had sometimes shared meals at the pub down the street with a couple of them, but by and large, they had been very surface friendships. With so much of her emotions tangled up in the ending of her engagement to Nate and trying to accept her diagnosis, she hadn't been interested in developing any real deep friendships. There had been two young girls who shared a flat who had traveled with her on a few of her jaunts. It had been nice to have company, but there had also been pressure to do what they wanted even when her energy levels hadn't been very high. In the end, it had just been easier to travel by herself and take her time based on how her body was doing on any given day.

"I made a few friends, but none like Megan."

"What does Megan think of your diagnosis?"

"It was an adjustment for her."

"Did she visit you?"

Lily bit the inside of her lip. "Yes. Every six months or so she'd come see me."

Hurt crossed Cami's face. "So she knew about your diagnosis?"

"Yes. At the time, she was the one I felt safest telling."

Cami's brows furrowed. "Why didn't you feel safe telling us?"

Lily took a deep breath, hoping she could put it into words in a way that Cami would understand. "I was afraid to need any of you. Around that time, all of you had stuff going on. You and Josh were touring. Laurel and Violet were busy with their families, and Jessa had the business she'd started up here with the B&B plus her gardens. And Will...well, he had his own heartaches to deal with. I didn't want to burden anyone." Lily looked down at her hands, smoothing the fabric of her pants with her fingertips. "And I think I was scared that no one would care. To be honest, the only person that I felt gave me any sort of priority in their life was Megan. I had no mother or father to care about me. No grandparents. Just siblings who were busy with their lives."

Lily felt Cami's hand on her arm.

"I'm sorry we made you feel like that, Lily. I do understand why you did though. I felt the same way when I left here right after graduation. It seemed like no one would care if I wasn't around. It was all lies though. Lies Satan used to divide our family."

Lily nodded. "I understand that a bit better now. But back then, I figured it was better to not tell people. Then I wouldn't be disappointed by their response or lack of it. If I did share it, then I might have had to face the reality of how unimportant I really was to everyone."

"Ah, Lily. I hope you know that we are all here for you now. Just say the word and we'll do what we can for you. Our family has been fractured for far too long. Having you home now is helping to heal that final fracture." Cami paused. "Wait. You said that only Megan gave you priority?"

"Yes, that's how I felt back then," Lily said with a nod.

"What about Nate?"

Lily sighed. "He had a lot of pressure on him from his dad to work long hours to build the business. He was often too tired to do anything for or with me. I knew that my illness would just create more stress for him as he tried to juggle his dad's demands along with the ones that came with my diagnosis."

"His dad's not around anymore," Cami pointed out.

"True. But he's still got a lot on his plate that needs his attention. I don't need to be adding to that. In fact, I'm trying to do what I can to ease it. Inasmuch as my body will allow me to."

Cami didn't respond right away, leaving Lily to wonder what was going on in her sister's mind.

"How do you feel about where you come priority-wise in people's lives now?" she finally asked.

"It doesn't matter to me anymore. Being on my own for the past couple of years has helped me to realize that I shouldn't be dependent on others for how I'm feeling about myself."

Cami nodded. "But just remember that you aren't an island unto yourself. We are here to support you as best we can. Don't rob us of the opportunity, sis."

Warmth filled Lily's heart. "I won't. In fact, I am going to need someone to do a little running around with me. I need to get a car. I'll be making trips into Minneapolis so want to have my own wheels."

"Are you able to drive still?"

Lily nodded. "I got the all-clear from the doctor I was seeing in London. He ran me through a bunch of tests for my vision and my reflex and response times. I'll most likely have to renew annually with a medical report to support being medically able to drive. I'm very aware of when symptoms are popping up that might prevent me from driving safely."

When Cami didn't reply, Lily glanced over to find her sister regarding her seriously. "What?"

"I'm just realizing how much you've grown up during the time you've been away. I can still remember the young girl I managed to con into taking me to the bar."

"Yeah, that wasn't very nice of you," Lily said as she reached out and playfully smacked Cami's arm. "Facing the wrath of the trio wasn't very fun at all."

"True, but you know, if I hadn't gone there that night, I'm not sure if things would have unfolded like they did with Josh. That was a turning point for us."

"Well, I'm glad that it turned out to be something good. I was so angry with you after that."

Cami grinned. "I know, but you forgave me."

"That I did. But you still owe me."

"Feel free to cash in at any time."

Lily stretched out her legs and then slid them off either side of the lounge. "Guess I'd better get back to work. I want to get a certain amount done before I call it a day."

"Yeah, I need to check on Jessa again. She was taking a nap when I left her. Don't say anything to her, but I think that baby is going to be here sooner rather than later."

Lily frowned. "How far along is she?"

"Thirty-four weeks, so technically the baby would probably be okay if delivered now, but every day he stays inside is better for him."

As they walked toward the porch steps, Lily said, "I admire how determined she is to stick to the bed rest."

Cami nodded. "She's gone to great lengths to protect this pregnancy."

"It will be nice to have a little one in the family again."

Cami opened the door and held it for her. "Yes, it will. I think we're going to stick close until he arrives. We have a couple of dates lined up, but each year we purposely make those concerts close so we can spend more time here during the summer."

Lily stopped for a glass of water while Cami put together some juice and fruit for Jessa's afternoon snack. Back in the library, she continued on with the task, methodically working through the invoices. They went back quite a few months, but hopefully within another day or two she would be all caught up.

"How's it going?"

Lily looked up to see Nate in the doorway. Her breath caught in her lungs as she watched him walk toward her. His faded jeans were grubby, and the t-shirt he wore had stains on it. Clearly he'd decided to put in some time under the hood of a vehicle or two at his shop. He wasn't a big man like Matt, but he still had the height of Lance and Josh, and was all wiry muscle. The perfect build for the work he loved so much...getting under the hood of a car and making it purr like a kitten.

"Everything okay?" Nate asked.

Realizing she'd been staring and hadn't answered his first question, Lily swallowed and glanced back at the screens in front of her. "Yep. Making pretty good progress, I think. It should be done in the next day or two."

The aroma of gas and oil drifted her way as he neared

where she sat. They were scents she would always associate with him. Her high school girlfriends had wrinkled their noses whenever he'd come around them after a day at work. The smell of the garage had clung to him, and his hands, though clean, still had stains on them. It had repulsed her friends, but to Lily, all of that represented the man she loved doing what he loved. He worked hard, which was more than she could say about the guys her friends chose to hang out with.

Nate settled on the corner of the heavy oak desk. "It will be a relief to have all that entered. With my year end coming up I need to get that up to date or my accountant will have a stroke."

"Do you have payments that need to be entered as well? I'm assuming you've paid these bills one way or another." Lily made the mistake of looking away from the screens and straight into his chocolate brown gaze.

"I hate to ask you to do more."

Don't do it. Don't do it.

"I don't mind. It's kind of like riding a bike. Once I got working on it, it all came back to me."

"If you're sure, I'll go to the bank tomorrow to see if I can get statements from them. All the ones I had were in the house."

"You should be able to get them from the bank website."

Nate lifted an eyebrow. "Really? I'm not too up on this. In the past, I just kept the copies the bank sent me and worked from those."

"If you trust me with your username and password, I'll get the information that way."

He stared at her for a few seconds before responding. "Of course I trust you."

Her heart clenched, and she had to work to keep her gaze on his, hoping all the while it didn't reveal the tumult of emotion going on within her. "Once I'm finished with the invoices, I will move on to that."

"I don't know how to thank you for all your help."

"No thanks necessary. It's the least I can do."

"What's the *most* you can do?" Nate asked.

This time she did look away from him. She twisted her hands together in her lap. As he sat there, the slight scent of motor oil clinging to him, Lily realized that she wanted nothing more than to be back in his arms. To feel his lips pressed to hers as his fingers tangled in her hair. To hear the strong, steady beat of his heart beneath her ear as he held her close. In all the upheaval of her life with Gran and then feeling a little set adrift once her older siblings began to find their own directions in life, Nate had been her rock.

If she didn't think that he deserved better than the life that lay ahead of her, she would ask him to give her a second chance. But he did deserve better.

"I'm happy to help out with the bookkeeping side of the business. To get you all caught up."

When he didn't respond right away, she looked at him and found him watching her intently. At one time, she would have been able to easily read his expression. But everything about him seemed closed off to her now. She told herself it was for the best, and yet that did nothing to ease the tight band around her heart.

He stood up and pulled his phone from his belt. After tapping the screen a few times, he handed it to her. "Here is the username and password for the bank site."

Lily took the phone from him, their fingers brushing. She picked up a pen and scribbled the information on the pad of paper she'd been using to make notes. As she handed the phone back to him, Lily wondered what his background photo was on his phone now. At one time, it had been a picture of the two of them.

She gave herself a mental shake. This was not a good path to be going down. Decisions already made needed to be upheld. She couldn't go changing things now when she knew that it wasn't right.

"I'll get the bank statements once I'm done with the invoicing." She rested her hand on the mouse and stared at the laptop screen.

"No rush. It's been sitting around this long. A few days won't make much difference."

Lily nodded. "I'll keep that in mind."

He put his phone away and said, "I'm going to go take a shower and get this garage smell off me before dinner."

Lily watched him walk away, remembering times when he would swing by to pick her up after he finished work. He'd be tired and dirty, but she was eager to spend time with him so she'd go with him to his house. There were times she would offer to give him a massage before he would shower. Many times. She knew now they had created an intimacy that had been more than it should have been between them. Part of their excuse had been that they were going to get married anyway. But she was proof now that engagements don't always end in marriage. To assume that as an excuse for taking intimacies had been wrong. They'd never taken that final step, but they'd gone much further than they should have, and now that led to memories which made things even more difficult.

There had been times over that first year when she'd wondered if the MS had been punishment for allowing things to go as far as they had with Nate. She'd known better. So had he. But after being together for so long, it had felt like the next logical step. Because, of course, before the diagnosis, marriage had been the destination.

As she turned her attention back to the invoices, Lily realized she'd made a big mistake in assuming that being around Nate would help them be just friends. Feelings she thought were gone had, in fact, just been dormant. Close proximity to Nate once again was bringing them all to the surface and there was nothing she could do about it. But she was still determined to help him out where she could because, as she'd told him, it was the least she could do.

❦

Head bent, Nate let the hot water beat down on his neck. Though it had left him sore, he was glad that he'd had a chance to do some work in the garage. It really was his true love when it came to the business. He'd learned about cars from the time he was old enough to safely be around when his dad worked on them. The administration and paperwork drove him nuts, but let him under the hood of any type of car, and he was a happy camper.

He hadn't been able to do much hands-on work since his dad's death. He'd been forced to shift his attention once his dad wasn't there to handle the business side of things. The weight of that responsibility had been heavy and stressful. It just compounded the loss he felt with both Lily and his dad gone.

Though he wished Lily were more receptive to reconsidering their relationship, Nate was grateful that at least she was willing to help him with the bookkeeping for now. Given what he'd heard Cami and Amy discussing earlier, he was pretty sure she hadn't been completely honest about why she'd ended things with him. Sure, she'd gone on to do her traveling, but he'd always wondered if there had been more to it. As far as he knew, her leaving hadn't been about another guy. He'd asked Megan about that one day when he'd allowed his heartbreak to override his common sense. She'd assured him there wasn't anyone else. The fact that Lily was back and alone seemed to support what Megan had told him.

Nate stepped from the shower and quickly dried off before pulling on fresh clothes that didn't reek of oil and sweat. His stomach rumbled as he debated shaving, but he left the bathroom without even picking up the razor. He was tired and couldn't care less what people thought about his several days' old stubble. Of course, he had to admit that knowing Lily had always liked him with a little stubble helped make the decision easier.

After picking up his phone, he headed back downstairs. The savory scent of supper greeted him as he reached the main floor. Instead of going to the library, even though he really wanted to, Nate walked into the kitchen.

❦ Chapter Eight ❧

*H*EY, Nate," Cami said as she looked up from the pot she was stirring on the stove. "Hungry?"

"Well, whatever you're cooking is making my stomach rumble." He wandered over to the counter and settled on one of the stools there. "Will around?"

"Yep. He's upstairs checking in on Jessa. Should be back in a few minutes." Cami set the spoon down and covered the pot. "How was your day?"

"I got my hands dirty, and someone else is dealing with the paperwork, so all in all, one of the better days I've had recently."

A smile flashed across Cami's face. "I'm happy to hear that. You deserve a good day after all you've been through."

"Hope I have more than one, but I still have lots to figure out with regards to my house and the garage in Sanford." Nate saw Cami's gaze go past him about the time he felt a hand on his shoulder. He glanced up, not surprised to see Will standing beside him. "Hey, man."

Will sat down on the stool next to him. "How's it going?"

As he repeated the conversation he'd just had with Cami, she busied herself making a salad.

"Have you decided yet if you're going to rebuild or not?"

Nate shrugged. "Part of me says no. Expanding was what my dad wanted. I'm content with just the one garage." He traced a pattern on the smooth counter-top. "I think it's time for me to leave room in my life for some...other things."

Will's eyebrows rose. "Things going that well with you and Crystal?"

Nate looked down at his hands. "No. She broke up with me on Sunday."

"Sunday?"

Nate lifted his head in time to see Will and Cami exchange a look. "Yep. Apparently she'd decided at some point that if she didn't feel I was fully committed to her by the time Lily came back, she would end things."

"Sorry to hear that."

"It's given me something to think about. I was so busy with the garages that I never really gave my relationship with Crystal much of a go. She did most the work arranging times for us to be together and such. Can't really blame her for not feeling like I was fully committed. Any other relationship I might have will be no different if I'm still tied up with both garages."

"Sounds like this might be an opportunity for you to change things so they're less stressful and demanding on you."

"Yes, but then I think of the guys over there who were working for me. They were good guys, and I'd like to give them their jobs back, but chances are they won't wait for me to rebuild. They can't. Several of them have families to support. So that would mean having to train a whole new staff." He shook his head. "I'm not sure I'm up to that."

"I don't envy you the decisions, but will certainly pray that God will give you wisdom."

Nate nodded though he wasn't really happy with God right then. "Will have to decide sometime in the next week or so."

He heard the front door open and glanced over his shoulder to see Lance walk into the kitchen. He'd barely had time to greet them when the door opened again. This time the arrival was much more raucous as Josh and Amy ushered several children into the kitchen.

"Whoa. Rowdy crowd," Lance said as he gave his daughter a hug. "I think I'm going to go check on Jessa."

"Chicken," Cami called out after him as Josh wrapped an arm around her waist and pulled her close for a kiss.

Amy came to stand next to Will where he sat and draped an arm around his shoulders. "That. Was. Nuts."

Will slid an arm around her as she leaned into him. "I did wonder what you and Josh were thinking."

"I can handle a class of fifteen or so students, but man, these kids ran us ragged."

"Where are Violet and Laurel?" Josh asked. "They said they'd pick up the kids here."

"I'm sure they're enjoying the peace and quiet in their houses," Will said with a grin. "They'll probably arrive at the last possible moment."

Nate had always found the sibling interaction of the Collingsworth family interesting. Given that he was an only child, he'd had no experience with brothers or sisters. He could tell that the relationships had grown and deepened over the years. He still had a clear memory of the night he'd gone into the bar to try and get Cami to come back to the manor. She'd certainly changed since that encounter.

"Hey, Lily."

Nate fought the urge to turn around when he heard Amy call out. He heard the kids greeting her and then she was standing on the other side of the counter.

Trying to keep his expression neutral, he said, "Done for the day?"

"Yes. Made a good dent in it."

She turned to Cami and said something that he couldn't hear. Since she stood between him and Cami, he didn't know what her response was, but right away Lily turned and walked slowly from the kitchen.

He looked at Cami. "Is she okay?"

Once again, he saw her exchange looks with Will and then Josh. "She's alright. She's just going to rest for a bit before supper."

Rest? That didn't sound like the Lily he knew. She'd always been full of energy, raring to go. He couldn't recall if she'd ever told him she needed to rest during the day. "What's wrong with her?"

Amy moved away from Will. "Hey, kids, why don't we go out back?"

Nate watched as Amy herded the kids out the back door. A pit formed in his stomach. Something *was* wrong with her. He could feel it. He looked at Cami and then at Will. "What's wrong with her?"

"She has MS, Nate," Will said.

"MS?" Nate asked, shock spreading through his body. "Multiple sclerosis?"

"Yes." Cami crossed her arms, her hands gripping the sleeves of the t-shirt she wore.

His chest tightened as if it were in a vise. Nate fought to take a breath. "Is that why...she left?"

"Yes, it was."

"Why didn't she tell me?" His heart broke again as he imagined Lily dealing with this diagnosis all on her own. "Did you know?"

"None of us did. Not until she came back. That's when she

told us." Cami came around the counter and slid an arm across his shoulders.

Weakened, Nate's head dropped forward as he tried to process this news. It wasn't because she hadn't loved him. It was so much worse. Right then, he wished it had been because she hadn't loved him anymore. At least that would have meant she was okay.

But why hadn't she told him? He would have been there for her. He'd already agreed to marry her, which would have been in sickness and health. Did she think he would have walked away when he found out? Surely she knew him better than that.

He felt Cami's arm slide from his shoulders and looked up. "How bad is it? I don't know anything about MS."

"None of us do," Will said. "We've all been trying to learn what we can about it. She's had almost three years to process and adapt to the news, it's going to take a while for the rest of us to catch up."

"The one thing she has told us is that it's very unpredictable," Cami added. "It could be years before she really experiences the more debilitating symptoms."

"Or it could be tomorrow?" Nate asked.

"Unfortunately, yes." Cami leaned against the counter, her expression pensive. "But it seems she knows what to look for and how to avoid situations that may exacerbate things. I think she's still recovering a bit from her trip here. It was long and draining on her."

Nate still couldn't believe what they'd revealed. "I wish she'd told me."

"She had her reasons for leaving and not telling any of us." Will sighed. "I can't say I agree with them completely, but it was her decision to make."

"We're just glad she's back home," Cami said.

Nate nodded his agreement. Home was where she needed to be while dealing with something like that. But what did he do with the knowledge? Did he confront her about it? Wait to see if she told him herself? "So what do I do now?"

"I told you just so you'd be aware. I don't think there's anything you need to do. She's still pretty set on the decisions she made three years ago being the right ones."

Nate knew Will was basically saying that she hadn't changed her mind about ending their engagement. For now, he'd respect her decision as he had for the past three years, but having learned this news didn't change how he felt about her. Until he'd heard the news, Nate had thought maybe his feelings for her weren't as strong as they'd once been. But the shock of finding out about her diagnosis had ripped that illusion away.

He loved her as much now as he ever had. Was it possible that she too still felt something for him? The thought that it might be caused a spark of hope to flare to life. He knew overt actions would likely cause her to retreat from him, but he could be subtle. Show her that he was there for her. Show her she was not alone. And maybe when she realized he wasn't going anywhere, she'd open her heart to him again.

༄༅

When her alarm went off, Lily debated shutting it off, rolling over and going back to sleep. The exhaustion that had plagued her in the days leading up to her departure from London had still not totally loosened its grip on her. She'd had to stop working on Nate's invoices earlier because she'd recognized the fogginess overtaking her brain for what it was. Though she'd basically come to terms with her diagnosis, she still got frustrated with the symptoms that prevented her from doing things the way she used to.

Moving slowly, she sat up and swung her legs over the side of the bed. She reached out to pick up the brush she'd set on the nightstand earlier and used it to smooth out the tangles from her nap. After finishing, Lily sat for a minute, bracing herself for having to deal with Nate again. Though her heart betrayed her by still feeling so strongly for him, it was times like this when the exhaustion and fogginess served to remind her why she'd ended things with him in the first place.

She wasn't the woman he'd fallen in love with. No longer could she go for long hikes or stay up super late without having to pay the consequences for that at some point. Such a large outlay of energy would require a time of recovery. Sometimes an extended one. Occasionally she did it, but she'd learned early on that it was better to keep a balance between activity and rest or she risked a relapse.

The trip home had put her on the edge of one which was why she'd tried to keep her physical activity to a minimum and get rest when she could. But for now, she needed to get herself onto her feet and down the stairs to eat dinner with the family. And though she wasn't super hungry, she knew that she needed a good meal to give her body the fuel it needed.

As she left her room, she spotted Lance coming from his and Jessa's suite.

"How is she?" she asked as Lance joined her at the top of the stairs.

"Hanging in there." He held his arm out toward her.

Grateful that he didn't make a big deal out of helping her, she slid her hand into the crook of his elbow and put her other hand on the banister.

"I hear you've been helping Nate with his paperwork."

"Yes. I know he struggles with that, and it's something I can do without expending too much energy."

"I'm sure he appreciates it. I'm glad I don't have to take care of that side of things with my company."

Once she stepped off the last stair, Lily slid her hand from his arm. She really didn't want to walk into the kitchen looking like she needed help to put one foot in front of the other.

The kitchen was crowded with everyone there now,

including their kids. Though she tried not to, Lily couldn't keep herself from scanning the room for Nate. She spotted him standing off to the side talking to Will. When his gaze caught hers, he stopped talking and just stared at her for a moment. He gave a little nod of his head then turned his attention back to Will.

Lily moved to stand against the wall for support, telling herself not to be disappointed by his quick acknowledgment and then dismissal of her.

It's what I want. Too bad her heart didn't agree.

Once Lance said a prayer for the meal, the parents moved toward the food on the counter to help the little ones load up their plates. After the kids had been ushered outside to eat at the picnic table, things quieted and the adults were able to get their food. Lily contemplated following them outside as well but had a feeling the day had only gotten hotter since she'd been out earlier with Cami. Once she had food on her plate, she sat down at the table.

Amy slid onto the chair across from her. "I'm going to stay here and enjoy a little quiet. After spending the day with those kids, I need it."

Lily smiled as she took a sip of her water. "I can only imagine. Something like that would completely wear me out."

"You staying in here, babe?" Will asked as he brought over his plate filled with food.

"Yeah, I was just telling Lily I'm gonna let the parents deal with their own kids for a while."

Lily was relieved when she saw Nate follow Matt out the back door. "I'm staying inside because heat doesn't really agree with me anymore."

Will settled into the chair next to Amy. "What happens if you are out in the heat?"

"It can trigger a flare-up of my symptoms if it's too intense. The big things for me are stress, getting overtired and heat."

"So I guess you're going to love winters now," Will said as he stabbed at a carrot on his plate.

"Love might be stretching it, but I'll definitely enjoy them more."

Lily ate some of the salad she'd taken, noticing as she did that Amy elbowed Will and gave him a look.

Will cleared his throat and took a drink from his cup. "Uh, I guess I should let you know that I told Nate about your MS."

✒ Chapter Nine ✑

*T*HE revelation stabbed her like a red hot poker. She'd known that Will would likely tell him at some point, but suddenly Nate's dismissal of her earlier made sense. Hoping her distress didn't show on her face, she said, "Guess he knows how lucky he was to have dodged that bullet now."

Amy frowned, her brows drawing together. "I didn't get that feeling."

"Well, once he decides to do a little research on how the disease can progress, he will feel that way."

Will reached across and touched her hand. "Are you mad at me?"

"No. I knew he'd find out sooner or later. It was probably better coming from you than anyone else."

"And I have to agree with Amy. I didn't get the feeling he was relieved that he wasn't engaged to you anymore because of it."

Lily shrugged. "It really makes no difference. I still believe I made the right decisions when I ended the engagement and left here. That time away was important for me."

"I can see that you've changed since then," Will commented. "I just don't want you to ever doubt that we're here for you now."

Though she knew it was natural that much of the conversations would go back to her disease during the first little while after her return, Lily did look forward to being able to talk about other things. It was still new to them, but the newness of the diagnosis had worn off for her.

"So are you planning to go back to Dallas?" Lily asked Amy.

Amy smiled as she looked over at Will. Lily's heart clenched at the look that passed between them. She was happy Will had found love again after losing Delia so tragically. And as she watched him and Amy interact, she noticed that he was much more relaxed and at ease than she remembered him being with Delia. And it was hard to miss how much Will's daughter, Isabella, adored Amy.

"For now I'm going to be hanging around Collingsworth. At least until Jessa's baby is born and they don't need me anymore." Amy grinned as she batted her eyelashes at Will. "Beyond that...well, we'll just have to see."

Before Will could respond, the back door opened. Lily looked over and saw Nate coming inside, plate in hand.

He approached the counter where the food was. "So this is where you guys are hanging out."

"Yeah, we're keeping Lily company," Will said. "Join us."

Lily shot Will a look. It was one thing that he'd decided to tell Nate about the MS, he didn't have to keep trying to get them together. It wasn't going to happen, and it would just make things awkward.

"Sure." Nate added some food to his plate and then sat down in one of the empty chairs at the table.

Lily was grateful he hadn't seated himself right next to

her. She pushed the food around on her plate with her fork before taking another bite of the salad. The knot in her stomach made it difficult to want to eat.

"So why are you inside instead of enjoying the nice summer evening?" Nate asked as he spread butter on a roll.

Will glanced at Lily, his eyebrows rising.

Swallowing the bite she'd just taken, Lily said, "My body doesn't do too well with heat anymore."

Nate lowered his fork to his plate. "Heat bothers you?"

Lily nodded, not meeting his gaze. She was pretty sure he was remembering all the times they'd done things together even on the hottest of days. Whether it had been going for a hike or riding bikes, she'd never hesitated to participate. Though they hadn't done it on a regular basis because of his other responsibilities, heat had never been a reason not to do something. However, it was something she had to factor into her decisions now.

"So you have to check the temperature every day?" Amy asked.

"Only if I'm planning to be outside for any length of time." With the conversation once again on her disease, Lily tried to suppress her frustration. Would the MS now define who she was in the eyes of her family? Would her limitations be all they would see?

Will pushed his now-empty plate away from him. "Are there days when you feel completely normal?" He leaned away from the table, slipping his arm across the back of Amy's chair.

"Normal isn't a word I use much to describe my days anymore." Lily moved her plate a few inches so she could lean her arms on the edge of the table. "But yes, there are days where I definitely feel like I could do more than I can on other days."

"How soon do you know what kind of day it's going to be?" Nate asked.

Against her better judgment, Lily looked at him. She thought she might see pity there, but right then, all she saw was concern. "It's usually something I determine as the day goes along." Though she wished for a different topic of conversation, she decided that the sooner they understood about it, the better. "I'll give you an example that might help you to understand how my days unfold. Imagine that at the beginning of your day you were given a dozen spoons. For each thing you plan to do that day, you must give up one spoon." She looked at Amy. "How would you spend your first spoons?"

"I guess I'd get up and get ready for my day. Take a shower. Do my makeup."

"Are you planning to wash your hair? Shave your legs? Because on certain days, those two tasks would each require a spoon. Then you'd do your hair and makeup. Two more spoons. Getting dressed. Another spoon. So you've spent five spoons, and you haven't even had breakfast yet. And if you're making your own breakfast that will be another spoon. You're halfway done with your spoons and the day has just started."

Amy's brows drew together. "Seriously? So you have to plan out your day like that?"

"Yes. Particularly when I'm dealing with stress or I'm overtired. There can be stretches of time where I'm able to get through my days without having to focus on my spoons, but that's usually when I've taken the time to balance my life. Get the rest I need. Eat a balanced, healthy diet. Take my medication. Get a little exercise."

"How many spoons did it take you to do what you did for me today?" Nate asked. He had leaned back, one arm on the table, the other hooked over the back of his chair.

"Barely one. Sitting like that doesn't require too much energy." Lily decided she might as well put it all out there. "I did have to stop though when my brain started getting a bit foggy."

"Foggy?" Nate moved forward, his brown gaze intent on her. "What do you mean?"

"It's just another part of the MS. Sometimes when I'm tired my brain goes a little...foggy. It's hard to describe. But usually it means I can't focus as well and tend to make mistakes. That's why I went upstairs to lay down before supper. Rest helped to lift that fog for the time being."

Nate's gaze held hers for a long moment before he said, "I wish you'd told me."

Lily glanced at Will and Amy, not sure she wanted to have this discussion with an audience. "I did what I needed to. I couldn't deal with everyone else's emotions about it when I was still trying to come to terms with it myself."

"I wasn't everyone else, Lily." His voice had a gruff edge to it, and though it wasn't a tone she'd often heard from him, Lily knew his emotions were stirred.

She swallowed hard. "I did what I had to."

"I'm sure none of us understand what that was like," Amy said, no doubt feeling the emotionally charged air between Lily and Nate.

Lily shot her a grateful look. "Having spent the last few years getting used to living with this disease makes it easier for me to tell you about it."

"You're going to get tired of the questions, aren't you?" Will commented.

"If you really want to find out more about it, I can give you a website to visit. Or just do a search for it." Lily paused then said, "I have been diagnosed as having the relapsing-remitting form of MS. There are lots of symptoms listed on the websites, but at the moment, I don't have all or even most of them. The thing to remember is that this disease is very unpredictable. I can be fine one day and have a relapse the next. And there are things called invisible symptoms. They're the ones you can't necessarily see that I might be dealing with.

"More than anything I just need people to trust that I know my limits. If I say I can't do something, even if I look fine, respect that I know my body can't handle it. I take medicine that helps keep the disease from progressing more quickly, and I also take medication to help with symptoms and things like pain. Though I may go for long stretches of time without my symptoms worsening or changing or having a relapse, I eventually will get worse. It's pretty much a given. Unless they find a cure..."

Lily pulled her plate back toward her and took another bite. The silence around the table was heavy, and she was sorry in a way she'd brought it down, but she needed them—Nate especially—to understand what lay ahead. She might look normal, but the disease was at work in her body, and sooner or later, her bad days would be more frequent than her good ones.

Several people came in the back door, stalling any further conversation. Lily focused on finishing up most of what was on her plate, completely aware of Nate sitting in silence so very close to her.

Amy stood up and reached for their plates, stacking them in front of her before carrying them to the sink. "Everyone ready for dessert?"

Lily declined but offered to take some up to Jessa. She needed to get away from the tension radiating off Nate. Though Lance had eaten dinner with Jessa, he left the two of them alone when she came bearing ice cream for his very pregnant wife.

Jessa seemed to sense that she didn't want to talk about herself. So instead, as Jessa enjoyed her dessert, they talked about the baby and all the things she looked forward to doing once she was off bed rest. As Lily looked at her eldest sister, she remembered the struggle she'd often had when it had come to her relationship with Jessa. Though not old enough to be her mother, it was the role she'd taken on for Rose and Lily when Gran had started to pull away near the end of her life. Most outside the family hadn't known it, but Rose had actually been Laurel's daughter, so Gran's death had allowed her to claim Rose as her daughter in a way she never had been able to before. That had left Lily. And finding out about their mother hadn't changed anything since Elizabeth hadn't been in any shape to be a mother to anyone, let alone an eighteen-year-old girl looking for that connection.

And then when Lance had come along, and Jessa's attention had been caught up with him and the renovations on the manor, Lily had felt as if she'd just been set adrift. Nate had been the only one who had stuck by her during that time. It had been difficult for her to accept all the changes. Looking back now, she could see how immature she'd been. How self-centered in wanting the attention for herself.

"Everything going okay with you, sweetie?" Jessa asked as she reached out to brush her hand along Lily's cheek. "And I'm not asking about the MS side of things. Just in general. Are you doing okay being back home?"

Lily rested back against the pillow and sighed. "There are a few adjustments, but I wouldn't want to be anywhere else. I'm glad to be home."

"And we're...I am glad you're home. I've missed you."

As they lay there together, Lily shared about her time in London. "I have lots of pictures I can show you."

"I'm so glad you got to experience that. I'm such a homebody that I'll just live vicariously through you." Jessa paused. "Are things okay between you and Nate? Are you finding it difficult to have him staying here?"

"It's okay. He's had some hard hits lately. I don't think a motel would be a good place for him. He knows about the MS now, so that's all out in the open."

Jessa's eyes widened. "You told him?"

"Not me. Will did."

"And you're okay with that?"

"Surprisingly enough, yes. It was going to come out sooner or later."

Laurel, Cami and Violet walked into the room, stalling

any further conversation.

"The guys agreed to keep an eye on the kids, so we're up here for some sister time before we leave," Violet said. They pulled chairs close to the bed and settled in. "So what's new?"

When Laurel and Violet left a little while later, Lily retreated to her own room without going back down the stairs. Though they once hadn't been a problem, too many times up and down them taxed the muscles of her legs and back.

Lily sat on the edge of her bed to judge her energy level. Did she have enough to take a shower tonight? It would be one less thing to have to do in the morning. One less spoon to use up the next day.

In the end, she decided to go ahead and use the last of her energy to take a shower since she had no idea what the next day would hold. When she lived in London, she controlled her day to day interactions and activities. Now that she was back at the manor, she could no longer plan out her days without regard for anyone else.

After the shower, Lily towel dried her hair but decided against blow drying it. If it was too wild in the morning, she'd just wear it up. Once in bed, propped up by pillows, she let out a long sigh before picking up her Bible and devotional book from the nightstand. She laid them on a pillow on her lap and opened the Bible to where a notecard marked where she'd left off the night before.

Though she'd always been told to have her devotions in the morning, Lily found she preferred the night. She read through the devotional passage for the day and the accompanying scripture. Afterward, she closed her eyes for a moment to try to clear the fogginess that still edged her mind. She looked down at the verse she'd printed on the notecard before leaving London. It was her verse for the week. She tried to memorize a verse each week, even when she struggled to remember things because of her brain fog.

The note card contained the verse she'd written down

from Deuteronomy. *And the Lord, He is the One who goes before you. He will be with you, He will not leave you nor forsake you; do not fear nor be dismayed.* As she'd prepared to make her journey back to her family, it was a verse that she had held tightly to. She'd had no idea what to expect when she returned, but knowing that God was going before her and wouldn't leave or forsake her had given her peace.

Once her time of memorization was done, she set the books back on the nightstand and snapped off the light. She found that if she spent the last minutes before she fell asleep thanking God for her day and focusing on the positive things instead of all the things that might have gone wrong through the day, it helped her relax and sleep better.

$\infty\sim$

Nate wished he'd been able to talk to Lily again once the meal was over, but she hadn't reappeared after going upstairs to spend time with Jessa. When her sisters had come back down, she hadn't been with them. He'd escaped to the library, not wanting to continue to intrude on their family time.

Sitting at the desk, he brought the laptop to life and spent a few minutes looking at what Lily had accomplished that day. Given what he now knew of her physical condition, he was very thankful she'd agreed to help him out. That she'd give up one of her spoons to do this work she knew he disliked so much touched him. He didn't know why she'd done it. And though he was trying not to attach too much significance to it, it still gave him some hope.

He shut down the accounting program and brought up a browser. After a moment's hesitation, he typed Multiple Sclerosis in the search engine. Nate recalled her saying what type she had, so he focused on what the pages said about that. He read about the symptoms and the challenges of life with MS. He read the pages and watched the videos that were available for the loved ones of the person diagnosed. He had a desperate need to understand what she was dealing with.

It was almost two hours before he sat back in the chair, heartsick. It hurt to think of what lay ahead for her. And it hurt that she hadn't felt she could lean on him when she'd first learned about her diagnosis. He would have been there for her. Had she doubted that? If anyone knew how to stick with someone who required care, it was him. He had seen his dad do it with his mom, and though it had been difficult at times, he knew his dad had never regretted it. Had Lily doubted his ability to do the same for her? And more than anything, he wondered how God could have allowed this to happen to her.

He reached out and clicked the mouse to shut down the browser. With a sigh, he stretched out his legs under the desk, lacing his fingers across his stomach. He wasn't convinced anymore that her ending their engagement had been because she didn't love him. Finding out about her diagnosis changed everything.

Unfortunately, while she may have loved him when she ended the engagement, there was no guarantee she still felt the same way. Almost three years had passed since that awful day. Had she gone on to have another relationship? Megan had said she hadn't left him because of a guy, but that didn't mean she hadn't found someone after she'd left. The thought didn't sit well with him, but he knew it wasn't fair to feel that way since he had done that very thing with Crystal.

Nate drew in his legs and pushed up out of the chair. He closed the lid of the laptop and left the library. The manor was quiet as he made his way to the kitchen to get something to drink and then upstairs to his bedroom. He paced the room a bit, missing his own home more than ever. He'd set up a gym in his basement and right then, he would have loved to have been able to work off some of the frustration and anger inside him.

Instead, he took a shower and then lay down to watch a bit of television before going to sleep.

❦

"I made several trips to Paris," Lily said as she pointed to the picture on the tablet Jessa held. "That was my second time."

"It's so beautiful." Jessa swiped the screen to the next picture. "I've never really wanted to journey too far from Collingsworth, but these pictures are making me think more about traveling. Of course, right now I'd be happy with being able to make a trip down the stairs."

"Your time will come soon enough." She reached out to touch Jessa's stomach, frowning when she felt it harden beneath her hand. "Is that a contraction?"

"Yes. Braxton Hicks. I'm having them fairly frequently now." Jessa sighed. "But thankfully they never develop into anything. Would like another couple weeks before the real deal."

As they continued through the pictures, Lily was glad that she'd decided to spend this time with Jessa instead of diving right into the work for Nate. She'd woken feeling a little sluggish and, after a trip downstairs to get something to eat, had decided to just lay low with Jessa for a bit.

"Maybe we could all go back there some day," Jessa said as they moved through a section of pictures Lily had taken in Scotland. "I know Violet for sure likes to travel."

"It would be fun to go as a group," Lily agreed. There had been several times she'd wished she could share the excitement of exploring new places with someone.

Jessa turned away from Lily, reaching out toward her nightstand. Suddenly she gasped, and the tablet slipped from her hands as she grabbed her stomach.

❧ Chapter Ten ❧

*J*ESSA?" Lily scrambled to get off the bed and around to the other side so she could see her sister's face. "What's wrong?"

Jessa panted for a few seconds before managing to say, "That one took my breath away."

Lily laid her hand on Jessa's stomach and felt the hardness there. It didn't ease away like the last one she'd felt. Her gaze met Jessa's, and she could see the fear there. "This is different."

Jessa nodded. "And I think my water just broke."

Lily jumped to her feet. "I'll be right back."

Yesterday Cami had stayed to make sure she and Jessa were okay even though Lily had insisted she could handle things. Now she desperately wished Cami or Amy—anyone—was still there at the manor. But she'd assured them she'd stick close to Jessa and they'd be fine while they took the kids to Laurel's.

Out in the upper hallway she glanced around. Noticing Nate's door was closed, she took a chance that he was still home.

She ran to his door and pounded on it with her fist. "Nate! Nate!"

Relief flooded her when she heard a muffled, "Hang on. I'm coming."

The door jerked open, and Nate stood there, concern written all over his face. "What's wrong?"

"Jessa said her water just broke. I think she needs to go to the hospital. I'm still not sure I should drive after my latest flare up, and no one else is here."

"Let me get changed," he said, motioning to the long, athletic shorts and muscle shirt he wore. "I'll be right there."

Lily nodded and raced back to Jessa's room. Her sister sat on the edge of the bed, her body bent forward. "Nate's still here. He'll take us to the hospital."

"Call Lance." The two words were edged in pain.

"Another one?"

Jessa nodded.

Sticking close to her, Lily pulled her cell phone from her pocket and quickly dialed Lance's number.

"Hello?"

Realizing that Lance probably didn't recognize her number, she said, "It's Lily. Jessa's water broke and we're taking her to the hospital."

There was silence on his end for what seemed like forever before he said, "I'm at a site about half an hour south of town. I'll meet you at the hospital as soon as I can."

After ending the call, Lily helped Jessa to the bathroom where she changed out of her wet clothes and into the dry ones Lily found for her. When they came back into the bedroom, Nate was standing in the doorway. "Ready to go?"

"Grab my bag, please, Lil," Jessa said, pointing to the closet doors. She held out her phone. "And put this in the pocket."

Lily hurried to the closet and found the bag sitting on the floor just inside the door. She picked it up and joined Nate, who had slipped his arm around Jessa's waist. Jessa leaned on him as they made their way to the stairs, pausing briefly so Lily could grab her purse. Halfway down, Jessa let out a groan, and Nate immediately stopped. Lily moved around in front of Jessa and together she and Nate held her as she breathed through the contraction.

Lily's gaze met Nate's as they waited for the tension to leave Jessa's body. She could see the concern there that was no doubt reflective of what was in hers.

Jessa took a deep breath and blew it out as she straightened. "Now I remember the pain."

Lily found her legs shaking as they continued down the rest of the steps.

Please, God, don't let my body fail me now.

But she knew that the stress of the situation combined with the exertion she'd already expended were not a good combination.

They helped Jessa to the rear door of Nate's truck. Jessa balked momentarily. "We should have grabbed a towel. I don't want anything to mess up your seats."

"Well, as long as you don't actually deliver, I think we'll be fine," Nate assured her.

Once Jessa was settled, Lily followed Nate around to the other side. "I want to get in back with her."

Nate nodded as he opened the door and then, just like he had so many times in the past, he reached for her. His strong hands gripped her waist as he lifted her into the truck. Though at any other time she might have protested the action, right then Lily was just grateful that she hadn't had to try to lift her legs high enough to get into his big truck.

"Why don't you call Dean and make sure his guys know not to pull us over on our way in. I'm going to come in from the west to avoid the traffic down Main Street."

"I don't have his number, but since I have to call Violet anyway, I'll tell her to pass the message on to Dean." After a glance at Jessa to make sure she was okay, she phoned Violet. "Vi, Jessa's gone into labor."

As with Lance there were a couple of seconds of silence before Violet said, "Okay, I'll line up babysitting with Laurel and Amy, and we'll be there as soon as we can."

"Do you want me to call Laurel?"

"No, I can call her. Why don't you call Will?"

"Okay." Then Lily passed on Nate's message. "We don't want to get stopped on our way to the hospital."

After calling Will with the news, Lily slid her phone into her purse and turned to Jessa. "The troops are all rallying."

Jessa gave a weak smile. "It's been a while since we rallied for this purpose."

"Well, I'm just glad you waited until I got home."

Tension tightened Jessa's features as her gaze lost focus. Lily moved closer to her and held out her hand for Jessa to hold. She tried not to wince at the strength in her sister's grasp. When the pain passed and Jessa's body relaxed, Lily asked, "Should I be timing something?"

"No, don't bother. With my water broken, they're not going to send me home. And once I get there, they're going to hook me up to everything that will tell them what's going on." Jessa gestured to her bag. "Actually, I forgot. I'm supposed to call my doctor."

Lily fished the phone out of the bag on the floor and handed it to Jessa.

"Hopefully, I can get through this before the next contraction," Jessa said as she touched the screen of the phone. "Hello. This is Jessa Collingsworth-Evanston. I'm on my way to the hospital. My water broke."

Apparently, whoever answered her call had been prepared for it because Jessa didn't have to say any more. She touched the screen again and then held the phone out to Lily.

"Are they able to handle an early birth?" Lily asked.

Jessa nodded. "The hospital has been working over the past few years to bring the NICU up to current standards. He'll be fine."

Lily was glad that Jessa wasn't going to have to stay in one hospital while her baby was whisked away to another. She knew it happened far too often.

As they got closer to Collingsworth, Nate said, "We've got company."

Lily glanced out the back window to see a cop car behind them. She met Nate's gaze in the rear view mirror.

"In the front, too," he said.

Lily looked between the front seats to see that another car led them, its lights flashing. "Guess we've got an escort to the hospital."

Jessa gave a soft chuckle. "Pays to be related to the sheriff."

"Or a member of the founding family," Lily added.

As they neared the city limits, another car joined the one in front of them and in addition to the lights came the sirens. Cars pulled over to allow them through, no doubt wondering who rated the special escort.

The cop cars continued on past the hospital, but Nate turned into the emergency entrance. He pulled to a stop where a small group of people waited with a wheelchair. One of them opened the back door even before Nate could get out. As they helped her sister from the back seat, Nate opened her door and held out a hand to help Lily.

He continued to hold her hand even after she was steady

on her feet. The warmth of his touch spread up her arm and into her heart.

I've missed this.

"Are you okay? I'm just going to park the truck, and I'll be back."

Lily nodded, hoping that she really would be okay, but not one hundred percent sure what her body might do. She rounded the back of the truck, willing her body to cooperate with the demands she would continue to put on it for the next little while. The group had already begun to move toward the automatic doors, and she followed as quickly as she could.

"Wait for my sister," she heard Jessa say.

One of the nurses moved to her side. "We're going to take her right up to labor and delivery."

Lily nodded and then followed them to the nearest bank of elevators. Jessa had another contraction as the elevator rose, and she reached out toward Lily. Grateful to still be of use to her sister, Lily stepped close to enfold Jessa's hand in hers. The doors slid open but since she was still in the midst of the contraction, one of the nurses held the doors open until it passed.

Since they skipped registration and headed straight into a large birthing room, Lily assumed that all the paperwork had been dealt with well in advance of this day.

"We're going to need to hook you up to some monitors," one of the nurses said as they helped Jessa onto the hospital bed. "Did the fluid appear clear when your water broke?"

"I think so," Jessa said. "I didn't notice any kind of staining on the bed or my clothes."

She glanced at Lily, who shook her head. "I didn't see anything like that either."

"Okay, good."

It wasn't long before the Violet, Laurel and Will showed

up, but it was Lance's arrival that finally eased some of the tension from Jessa's expression.

"Babe," Lance said as he rushed to Jessa's side. He took one of her hands in his and brushed a strand of auburn hair from her face. He pressed a kiss to her forehead. "Everything is going to be okay."

Lily saw their gazes lock and Jessa nodded. "Yes. Everything is going to be fine."

She swallowed hard as she watched their united front. It was as if in coming together they had just become a force to be reckoned with. They were going to face this side by side and would be together regardless of the outcome.

"I hate to do this," a nurse near the monitor said, "but I need to just have Jessa and Lance here for a bit until we get an idea of how the labor is progressing. We can have one other person beside Lance here for the delivery, but we will also have a neonatal team on standby so there won't be room for anyone else."

Violet and Laurel each approached Jessa to give her a kiss and assure her of their prayers. Will clapped his hand on Lance's back before giving Jessa a kiss as well. "We'll be in the waiting room if you need anything."

As Lily moved to follow them, Jessa grabbed her arm. "Do you want to be here?"

"I'm not sure if I'll be much help."

"Go rest now," Jessa told her. "Then come back when it's almost time, okay? I would like you here."

Tears pricked Lily's eyes. "If you're sure."

"We are," Lance said. "I'll come get you when it's time."

Lily left the room, eager to get to the waiting room so she could sit down. Her feet felt heavy as she walked in the direction indicated by the signs. She was almost there when she didn't lift her foot high enough and the toe of her shoe snagged on the carpet. Lily stuck her hand out to the side toward the wall, but it was a pair of strong arms that stopped her fall.

The familiar scent told her who it was before she looked up into a concerned brown gaze. "Are you okay?"

"Lily?" Violet was the first of her sisters to reach her. "What's wrong?"

Nate still held her in his arms, and Lily didn't have the strength to fight him. If all of this had transpired after she'd been home a few weeks, her body likely wouldn't have been reacting like this. However, coming so soon on the heels of the stress and strain of packing up her apartment and traveling back to Collingsworth, it was more than her body could be expected to handle.

"I'm okay. Just the way my body is sometimes now."

"Let's get you to a chair," Nate said as he swung her up into his arms. Before she could protest, he carried her to the waiting room and set her onto a chair there.

"Thank you," Lily said, keeping her head bent.

Emotions rolled through Lily, each warring for the upper hand. Worry for Jessa. Anger at the weakness of her own body. Frustration that she'd had to rely on Nate. And then there was the part of her that had relished being in Nate's arms once again. Even when her body hadn't been so weak, she had always enjoyed his strength. Whether it was lifting her into his truck or carrying her on his back when they'd go hiking. She had enjoyed being the weaker one in their relationship. Now, however, she hated the weakness.

"Are you okay?" This time is was Laurel who asked.

Lily tightened her hands. What she would give to never hear that question again. She had hardly heard it at all while away in Europe because no one knew. Something told her that every time she faltered, she was going to hear it now. "I'm fine. Right now, we need to be focusing on Jessa. Not me."

Laurel must have heard the hard edge to her voice

because she settled on the seat next to her, gave Lily a quick one arm hug and said, "You're right."

When Lily looked up, her gaze met Nate's. His concern was still very clear.

Don't pity me. Do not feel sorry for me. That's what she wished she could say to him. The very last thing she wanted from him was pity.

Thankfully, the arrival of Cami, Josh and Amy took the attention away from her.

"How's Jessa?" Cami asked.

As they filled her in, Amy went to stand next to Will, pressing against his side when he slid his arm around her. *I remember doing that with Nate.* Lily closed her eyes, took a deep breath and let it out. She needed to get herself under control. Thanks to the MS, her emotions were more near the surface than they used to be and at a time like this, it was hard to keep them in check.

She bent her head, keeping her eyes closed and focused on her breathing. If Jessa really did want her in that delivery room with them, she needed to calm herself.

In. Out.

In her mind, she pictured her favorite spot of the past three years. The chalet in Switzerland that she'd rented for a couple of weeks one winter and then for three weeks the next. The big rustic bed had been wonderfully comfortable and waking up to see the beauty of God's creation just outside the big glass windows had been incredible. She'd spent most her evenings curled up in front of the fire, a mug of hot chocolate in her hands, listening to her favorite music. Sometimes she'd read. Sometimes she'd prayed. Sometimes she'd let herself take a journey of what-if. And sometimes she'd cried. But mostly she'd been at peace there.

It was that peace she wanted right then.

Another deep breath in and out.

Conversation swirled around her, but she tried to block it out for just a few minutes. Long enough to calm herself and focus on what was really important.

Jessa. The baby.

Please, God, let everything be okay.

"Everybody doing alright at the house?" Laurel asked.

Slowly Lily lifted her head but was careful not to look in Nate's direction. Instead, she watched as Cami sat down next to Laurel.

Cami nodded. "Rose was just leaving for work when we got there, but the two babysitters had arrived. Hope they can handle everyone."

Laurel smiled. "They'll be fine. They do a great job with the kids."

"Hey, Lance." Will's greeting turned Lily's attention to the entrance to the waiting room.

Lance came right to where she sat. "Jessa wants you."

Laurel turned to her. "Are you—"

Lily raised a hand to cut her off. "I'll be fine."

When Lance held out his hand, she took it and then slid her other hand into the crook of his arm. Though she was sure he was in a hurry to get back, she appreciated that he shortened his stride.

"Is she doing okay?"

"So far. She's had an epidural. They're monitoring her blood pressure, but she's already dilated to six centimeters."

Lily glanced at Lance. "Isn't that rather fast?"

"Seems to be. From what I remember from Jessa's labor with Julia, it took her hours to get to this point."

When they reached the room, Lance found a stool for her to sit on next to Jessa's bed.

"Hey," Lily said as Jessa opened her eyes.

Jessa smiled, reaching for her hand. "Glad you're here."

❧ Chapter Eleven ❧

NATE stared down the hall where Lily had disappeared with Lance. He wasn't sure what to do. Part of him wanted to stay. If he hadn't been there earlier, Lily would have fallen. He wanted to be there in case she needed help again. But he knew he really had no right to be there. He wasn't family. He wasn't even a super close friend, though Will did trust him to work on his Escalade—which said something. Realistically, his tie to the Collingsworth family had been severed when Lily ended their engagement.

Bracing his hands on his knees, Nate stood up.

"You heading out?" Will asked.

"Yeah. I'm going to go to the garage for a bit. Let me know if you need me to do anything." He touched the phone on his belt. "Just call my cell."

Will stood and walked over to him. "You're welcome to stay and wait with us."

Nate glanced at the others, and each one nodded. "Thanks, but I think it would be easier for Lily if I wasn't here."

Will frowned. "If you're sure..."

"I am. I'll check in later. If I can bring you guys

anything—like food that isn't from the hospital cafeteria—let me know."

As Nate left the waiting room, he remembered how it had felt to be part of that group. For seven years, they'd included him as one of the family. But then he'd lost that. And then he'd lost the last member of his own family. Now it was just him. And from the looks of things, that wasn't going to change anytime soon.

Which was fine, he told himself. There were too many things demanding his attention right then. A relationship would just have suffered.

As he stepped out of the hospital, the warmth of the day embraced him. Remembering Lily's words about the heat, Nate hoped it didn't get too hot. It seemed her body was already struggling with the demands the day had placed on her.

Revving his truck's engine before putting it into gear to leave the parking lot, Nate gave a frustrated shake of his head. Couldn't he keep from thinking about her for even a minute? Every single thing lately seemed to lead back to Lily. Although, if he were honest with himself, he had to admit that over the time since she'd left, she really had never been too far from his thoughts. At least once a day something would bring her to mind. It was no wonder Crystal had felt he'd never fully committed to their relationship.

Walking into the garage, Nate saw a man in a suit talking with Don. No doubt someone from the insurance company. They'd said they would be stopping by. He'd assumed they'd let him know first, but apparently they hadn't felt the need.

"Mr. Proctor?" The man stuck his hand out as Nate approached. "I'm Steven Baylor."

He confirmed Nate's suspicions when he named the company he worked for. "What can I do for you?"

As the man began to talk, Nate found he was grateful for the distraction and was happy to give him his full attention.

❧

"Get her onto her left side," a nurse barked out. "We need to get her to the OR."

Lily pressed against the wall, panic flooding her as she watched the flurry of activity around Jessa. The nurses called back and forth as they disconnected and reconnected monitors. Things had been going okay until the baby's heart rate had dropped. Now they were scrambling to get her prepped for a move. Lily assumed it meant they were going to have to do a C-section.

Worry tightened Lance's features. As they pushed the bed out of the room, Lily caught a glimpse of Jessa's face. Her eyes were closed, and her skin was pale. Then the next moment, the bed with Jessa, the nurses, and Lance were gone.

Dear God, please protect them both. Please don't let anything...

When her trembling legs gave way, Lily slid down the wall and buried her face in her hands, struggling to draw in a deep breath past the vise that gripped her chest.

"She's in the best care." A hand rested on her shoulder.

Lily looked up and through moist eyes saw the face of one of the nurses who had been in and out of the room before everything had gone crazy.

"Let me help you," the woman said. She held out her hands to Lily.

"I have MS," Lily told her as she grasped them. "My legs aren't working too well at the moment."

"That's all right. I'll help you." The smile the nurse gave her was comforting. "Is the rest of your family here? In the waiting room?"

"Yes."

"Then let's go tell them what's transpired, okay?"

The nurse continued to reassure her as they slowly walked to the waiting room. Everyone surged to greet them once they spotted Lily.

"Is the baby here?"

Lily sank down into a chair and smiled her thanks at the nurse. "No. The baby's heart rate dropped. They had to take Jessa to the OR."

"She's going to have a C-section?" Laurel asked.

"It's a possibility," the nurse said. "It's a precaution if your sister can't deliver the baby quickly. They are both in excellent hands." She looked again at Lily. "I know it was a bit overwhelming to be in there when all of that was going on. But rest assured, it was just everyone doing their job to make sure of the best possible outcome for your sister and the baby. Someone will be out as soon as there is news."

"Thank you," Lily said. "For explaining and for helping me."

"You're welcome." The nurse gave them one last smile before leaving the waiting room.

Once she was gone, Laurel and Cami sat on chairs on either side of Lily. "How was Jessa?"

"Calm, but worried. Lance was, too."

"Why don't we take the time to pray for them right now?" Josh suggested.

As one by one they joined hands to close their family circle, Lily felt tears spring to her eyes. She bent her head as Josh began to pray. Tears dripped onto her legs, but she didn't release the grip she had on Cami or Laurel's hands.

"Father, we are so grateful for Your presence here today as Jessa and Lance face this emergency with their baby. We know You are there in that room with them and those who are caring for Jessa and the baby. We ask You to give wisdom to those making decisions and guide the hands of those administering care. We love Jessa and Lance and their little one. Please give them peace, and we ask that you allow their baby to be brought safely into this world. But in everything, we thank You for Your blessings and know that none of this has taken You by surprise. In Jesus' name."

"Amen." Each person there joined Josh in ending his prayer.

Lily took a shuddering breath before releasing her grip on her sisters. She rubbed her hands across her cheeks, and then, before anyone could ask, she said, "I'm not okay, but I will be fine."

"Are you sure?" Cami asked.

Even as Lily nodded, she hoped she was. Unfortunately, with each episode like this, there was always a chance she wouldn't come back fully from it. All she could do was take her medicine, get into see the doctor and rest up.

As she looked around the room, Lily realized that Nate was missing. She didn't want to acknowledge the disappointment that flooded her, but it was impossible not to. Trying to put a positive spin on his absence, Lily told herself she should be glad he hadn't been there to see the mess she'd been in when the nurse had brought her to the waiting room.

She leaned back in the chair, trying to ignore the tingling in her legs. Everything over the past couple of days had really opened her eyes to what it was like to live with MS while having people so intimately involved in her life. She truly had been in seclusion in London, doing only what she wanted to, when she felt able to do it. Suddenly her life was intertwined with everyone else's, and things happening to them could put demands on her body whether she was up to dealing with it or not. It was going to take some time to adapt to this.

Though she had come to accept her diagnosis, there were still moments when she was frustrated with it. She had learned to adapt her schedule if one day she didn't feel up to what she had planned. However, for the first time since those early days, Lily found herself more frustrated and agitated by the MS. And angry about it. She hated her body right then.

Hated the disease that was wreaking havoc on her relationships with her family as it already had on her relationship with Nate.

I want to leave.

Even as the thought came, Lily pushed it aside. Running away again was not the answer. It might have worked three years ago, but it wouldn't now. No, she needed to pull herself together and figure out how to adjust to this new normal, just as she had back when she'd finally come to terms with her diagnosis.

I can do this. That was what she had to keep telling herself. *I can do this.*

You are not alone.

The words rang so clearly that Lily actually glanced around to see who had spoken to her, but no one looked as if they'd just said anything. Then the words she'd written on her note card came to mind once again. *And the Lord, He is the One who goes before you. He will be with you, He will not leave you nor forsake you; do not fear nor be dismayed.*

She took a breath and let it out. Slowly her body was calming. The tingling was still there, but the trembling had eased. Lily wasn't sure she could run anywhere, but she could probably walk if she had to. With a little help. Movement in the hallway caught her attention and she looked over to see Lance coming towards them. As the others stood, she grasped Will's outstretched hand and allowed him to pull her to her feet. He settled her hand into the crook of his arm and then pulled Amy close with his other arm.

"How is Jessa? How is the baby?" The questions were fired at Lance as he came to a stop in front of them.

"Jessa is fine. They didn't end up having to do the C-section as she was able to push him out quickly. So far, he is doing okay. He's small though. Just about four and a half pounds. They've taken him to the NICU. After they're finished with Jessa, she'll go to her room."

"What's his name?" Cami asked.

"To be honest, we haven't completely settled on a name yet. I think we were both afraid to decide on a name in case it kind of gave him permission to come. Now we'll have to make up our minds quickly."

"Can we see Jessa?" Violet asked.

"Yes. Once she's settled." Lance rubbed a hand over his face. "I'm going to go back to her now. I'll come get you when she's ready for visitors."

Laurel hugged him. "Tell her we love her."

"I will." Lance smiled. "Thanks, guys."

The time between when Lance left and when they were able to go see Jessa seemed to drag on forever. They didn't stay long when they were finally able to see her. Jessa's exhaustion was evident on her face, and Lily knew that she probably needed rest with everything they were likely to face in the coming days. They assured her of their prayers and promised to be back later.

The heat of the day hit Lily like a punch as they walked out of the hospital. That was the last thing she wanted to deal with on top of everything. Thankfully Will's SUV cooled quickly as he drove her and Amy to the manor. Josh and Cami were going to Laurel's and would pick up Isabella along with their two girls.

Once at the manor Lily excused herself and slowly climbed the stairs to her room. She took her medicine and then lay down, sighing with relief to be in the cool of her room and finally able to relax her body.

Jessa was okay.

The baby was okay.

Thank you, God.

Tension flowed out of her as she closed her eyes and let the control she'd been desperately hanging on to disappear. It no longer mattered if her legs didn't respond to her needs.

It no longer mattered if they trembled. It no longer mattered if the tears she'd held in finally slid down her cheeks. No one was there to see and ask if she was okay. And right at that moment, she was fine with that.

✌⌒✍

As Nate walked into the manor, muscles he hadn't used in ages screamed at him. He tried his best not to limp, but it was a challenge. There was the pulsing coming from his temple, and he wouldn't be surprised if his nose was broken. But overriding it all was a strange sense of satisfaction.

Before heading upstairs, he went into the library to check something on his laptop. He pulled up short when he spotted Lily sitting behind the desk. For some reason, he'd figured she'd be in bed the rest of the day.

"Hey."

She looked up as he approached the desk, her green eyes large behind her glasses. "Hi. I was just trying to get a little bit more done on your stuff..." Her eyes widened. "What happened to your face?"

"Had a run-in with an arsonist."

"Your arsonist?"

"Yep. Punk decided to revisit the crime scene for some reason. I took off after him when I recognized who he was. He gave me a bit of a run, but I knew the neighborhood better than he did and caught him in a dead end back lane." Nate touched the side of his head then his nose. "He got a couple good licks in, but the cops were quick on the scene and took him off my hands."

Lily stood up and came around the desk. She looked at him closely. "You should probably get that looked at."

She reached out toward his face, her expression unreadable. Nate grabbed her wrist before she made contact. He stared at her, willing her to give him something—anything—to show that she still cared. He rubbed his thumb along the inside of her wrist, the smoothness of her skin a reminder of times past. She tugged her arm, and immediately he released her. "It'll be fine."

She stared at him for a moment before turning away and returning to her seat.

Nate moved to lean against the corner of the desk and studied her. He didn't like the pallor of her face nor the dark skin beneath her eyes. "There's no rush to finish this. You've had quite an eventful day. You should probably be resting." He saw her lips tighten and knew he'd said the wrong thing.

She turned her head back to the screens in front of her. "I did lie down for a while. This work isn't really taxing for me. Plus, Cami and Amy wouldn't let me do anything to help with supper."

He heard the thread of frustration in her voice. "I'm sure they're just concerned for you. Don't want you to overdo things."

Lily shot him a look that he couldn't read, but figured it was probably a good guess that she was frustrated with him as well. Perhaps keeping his mouth shut would be the better course of action at this point.

"I understand that. But it's already getting old being asked if I'm okay all the time." She lowered her hands from the keyboard to her lap. "The reality is that I'm not okay. I will *never* be okay. I have a disease that will slowly lay waste to my body as the years go by. Some days will be better than others. Some weeks or months will be better than others. But usually, when push comes to shove, in situations like I faced today, my body is more likely than not going to fail me."

Her words struck at Nate's heart like a sledgehammer. "So what are we supposed to do? When we are concerned and worried. What are we supposed to say?"

"You don't have to say anything," she said, her voice low. "I'm not your responsibility."

"That doesn't stop me from being concerned," Nate replied, trying to keep his voice normal even though her words once again wounded him. Aching from the inside out, he waited until she looked at him. "It doesn't stop me from caring."

Her brows drew together as she turned away from him once again. She kept her arms tight to her sides, hands clasped together in her lap. Nate wanted to reach out and pull her close, to cradle her to his chest and will his strength into her body, but he knew that would not be well received.

Nate put a hand on the desk and leaned toward her, trying not to wince as the movement pulled at a bruise on his ribs where the kid had managed to land a couple of punches. "Listen, Lily, you've had almost three years to adjust to this diagnosis. The rest of us are trying to catch up. Cut us a little slack while we figure it all out. If we ask if you're okay, just be honest with us. We all lo—care about you and are just concerned." He braced himself for her reaction to his near slip, but instead she just sat there stiffly. Then, to his surprise, her shoulders slumped and her head bent forward.

"I know. I'm sorry. I will try to be better about it. I'm just not used to having to explain my current health status to people on an hourly basis. For the past few years, most of the people I was around didn't know. I chose not to tell them so they didn't wonder when I tripped if something more serious was wrong. They just assumed I was clumsy."

Nate knew he shouldn't ask the question, but he couldn't help himself. "You weren't close enough with someone who would have noticed?"

She glanced at him and their gazes locked for a second before she shook her head and looked away.

At that moment, Nate just wanted to reach out and give her a shake. Something to wake her up and make her realize that he would be there for the long haul. If she'd only give him a chance. At times he thought she might still feel something for him, but if she did, it was clear she was fighting it.

Surprised she'd talked this freely with him but also a little afraid of saying something wrong, Nate leaned forward and closed the lid of the laptop. "Don't do any more work today. Enjoy this special time with your family."

Then, before she could say anything else, Nate stood up and left the room. Figuring Lily would be more comfortable without him around—and therefore have less stress—Nate went to his room to take a quick shower and then headed into town. Not in the mood for fast food, Nate went to Elsa's Café on Main Street.

❧ Chapter Twelve ❧

*T*HOUGH her husband had passed away a couple of years earlier, Elsa still bustled around making sure everyone who passed through the doors of her café left happy.

"Nathaniel!" Elsa came around the counter and grasped him by the shoulders to pull him down for a kiss on each cheek. "I'm so sorry to hear about your garage and house. But you're okay. That's the most important thing."

"Can't argue with you there," Nate said with a smile. "And no one else was hurt either."

"They catch the ones who did it yet?"

Nate nodded and pointed to his face. "I actually got to help with that." He gave her a quick recap of what had happened.

"Good." Elsa gave a firm nod of her head. "People like that need to face the consequences of their actions."

She led him over to a booth and after he was seated said, "You need a menu? Pot roast is the special tonight."

"Sounds good to me." After she had left, Nate leaned back

in the booth, stretching his legs out. He pulled his phone out and scrolled through email and social media while he waited.

"Hey, Nate."

Nate looked up, surprised to see Megan standing next to him. He straightened, setting his phone on the table. "Hi, Meg. How's it going?"

"Good." She gestured to the other side of the booth. "Can I sit down for a few minutes?"

"Sure. Have you eaten?"

She shook her head as she sat down, her eyes widened when she looked at him. "What's with the face? Lily didn't clock you, did she?"

Nate laughed. "She's never hit me before. I doubt she'd start now—even if she wanted to." He gave her the short version of what happened. "So what are you doing here?"

"I was across the street and saw you. Just wanted to see how you were doing. What with everything going on."

"By everything I assume you mean the fires and Lily coming home?"

Megan nodded, her red curls dancing with the movement. She regarded him seriously. "I'm sorry you're having to deal with so much at one time."

"I know about the MS, too."

Megan's light blue eyes widened. "Lily told you?"

He shook his head. "Will did. He figured I should know."

She nodded. "I thought you should, too. Lily felt differently."

"I guess I was in good company since none of her family knew either." He tilted his head. "But you knew."

"Not at first. Like everyone else, I was trying to figure out what happened when she broke off...your engagement and took off for Europe."

"But eventually she did tell you," Nate pointed out.

"Yes. I basically forced her to. I told her I was coming to visit her and flew to London. She had no choice but to tell me how to get to her place. She was a bit of a mess so it didn't take too long to get the truth from her."

"It was a shock. Of all the scenarios I'd run through my head, that hadn't been one of them. After all, she was young and, by all indications, healthy."

Before Megan could reply, Elsa appeared at the booth. She set a plate in front of Nate and another in front of Megan.

Megan smiled at the older woman. "Thanks, Elsa."

Elsa laid a hand on her shoulder. "You're welcome. I'll send someone with drinks for you."

Though it felt a little awkward, Nate offered to pray for their meal. Once they were done, a waitress approached them to bring them water and asked if they wanted any other drink.

"I'm good with the water, thanks." Nate picked up his fork as Megan also declined a drink. "Did you hear that Jessa had her baby?"

"No, I didn't. Is everything okay?"

"Cami said that aside from just being small, he looked good. He'll have to stay in the hospital a bit." He cut a piece of meat and said, "I'm surprised Lily didn't let you know."

"I've been giving her a bit of space to get reacquainted with her family. I'm the easy one to be around since I've known about the MS longer. She needs to learn to be around her family."

"Today was a rough day for her." Nate frowned at the memory. "She had difficulty walking, I think."

Megan nodded. "It seems that's something she struggles with when she gets overtired or stressed."

"Have you been around her when she's been like this before?"

"No, but she told me about it. That was early on. It seemed that she learned to read her body pretty well and had relatively few symptoms or relapses brought on by her own actions."

"Yeah, this was out of her control today."

Megan lifted her glass and took a sip, her gaze curious as she watched him. "You seem to know a fair bit about how she's handling things."

"Once Will told me what she was dealing with, I made it my business to be informed. And she also explained to us a little bit about how she faces each day. I know something about dealing with a debilitating illness day in and day out, but with my mom, each day just seemed to be progressively worse once she got past a certain point. There were no good days after that."

They ate in silence for a few minutes. Nate was curious as to why Megan had sought him out. Though she and Lily had been best friends, he and Megan had never become buddy-buddy. So her coming to him when Lily wasn't around was kind of odd. Finally, he just came right out and asked her.

She pushed her food around on her plate. When she eventually looked at him, he couldn't read her expression. "I was just concerned."

"Concerned? For Lily?"

She hesitated then shook her head. "For you."

Nate sat back. "Me? Why are you concerned for me?"

"I don't want you to get hurt again." Megan bit her lip. "Lily is very determined not to pick things back up with you. I don't want you to get your hopes up."

Nate had to admit, her words didn't sit well with him. In fact, they stung more than a little. He really had hoped that Lily would give them a second chance. "Why is that?"

"Her reasons are her own. I won't divulge them even if I don't one hundred percent agree with them. I just want you to be aware. If you two weren't living in such close proximity I wouldn't be as worried." Megan frowned. "Just...be careful."

"So how do I deal with her then?" Nate wasn't going to give up hope, but he didn't want to frighten her away by being too aggressive. Somehow he just wanted to show her that her diagnosis didn't scare him off, and he was going to be there for her...however she wanted him in her life.

"Don't try to do things for her. She needs to show that she's still capable of taking care of herself."

Nate gave a shake of his head. "That's the ironic thing. I used to take care of her all the time. I did things for her because I loved her and wanted to do them. I always carried her bags. I lifted her into the truck since it was a high step for her. I pushed the cart whenever we'd go shopping. Now she would view those same things as me taking away her independence. All because of a diagnosis."

Megan smiled ruefully. "Yes, that's kind of what's happened. I don't understand the mental side of it all that much. I've just kind of let her take the lead and let me know when she needs me to do something."

Their conversation turned to other things as they finished their meal. Megan reached for her purse, but Nate said, "I've got this. Thanks for saving me from having to eat on my own."

"You're welcome. I just wish I'd had a better reason." She slid to the edge of the booth and stood up. "Thanks for the dinner."

Nate watched her walk away, his mind going over what she'd said. When Elsa returned a few minutes later, he handed her enough money to cover both meals plus a tip and then left the café. Though she hadn't told him what he wanted to hear, perhaps it was still something he could put to use.

Because he wasn't going to give up on him and Lily just yet.

༈

Though the family members weren't able to see or hold the baby, Lance had some pictures on his phone that he showed them. Lily fought back tears when she saw the tiny little body hooked up to monitors and not where he should be. Which was in his mother's arms. Though Jessa had cried a few times during their visit, Lily knew that in the days ahead, her sister and Lance would be strong. They would stick together to do what had to be done for their little guy. And they were all very aware that it could have been so much worse. He could have had more problems than he did. For that, Lily was very grateful.

"So? You guys name the little dude yet?" Will asked from where he sat.

Tonight is was just the siblings and Lance in the room. The spouses—and Amy—had agreed to watch the children so they could go see Jessa.

Lance settled on the bed next to Jessa. "It took a little discussion, but I think we've come to an agreement."

They exchanged a look before Jessa said, "We've decided to name him Daniel Joshua."

A smile lit up Cami's face. "Josh will be so honored."

"Well, I am just relieved to not have to call him baby boy anymore," Violet said with a grin. "It might have stuck and then we'd probably end up with a rapper or something on our hands."

Lily was glad to see a smile on Jessa's face even if it was a small one. They didn't stay long since Lance and Jessa wanted to have a chance to see the baby again before Lance left for the night.

Violet and Laurel had brought their own cars, but Cami and Lily had come with Will. The drive home was quiet. Lily was still feeling the exhaustion the day had brought her. She longed for her bed and knew she wouldn't be staying up long once they got to the manor.

She saw Nate's truck in the driveway as Will pulled around to park in front of the steps. Lily slid off the seat and paused for a moment to make sure she was steady before she walked up the steps and into the manor with Cami. Nate wasn't in the kitchen, but instead of joining the others there, Lily told Cami she was going to her room.

Cami opened her mouth, closed it for a second and then said, "Sleep well. See you in the morning."

Lily hugged her, appreciating the effort she'd made to not ask her if she was okay. "Yep. See you in the morning."

She headed to the stairs but then veered to the right toward the library. It wasn't to see if Nate was there, she told herself. But that didn't explain why her heartbeat kicked up a notch when she saw him sitting at the desk. She was about to step back out of the doorway when he looked up and spotted her.

He stared for a moment, almost as if not sure she was really there. Then he smiled and said, "How was the visit with Jessa and the baby?"

"It was good." Lily ventured to the chairs on the near side of the desk. He moved the laptop over which gave her a clear view of him. "We didn't get to see the baby, but Lance had pictures. Jessa seemed a bit weepy, which isn't really like her, but completely understandable, of course."

Nate nodded. "Must be nice to have a baby in the family again."

Lily looked away from Nate. If things had gone as they'd planned, they would have had a child of their own by now. She pressed a hand to her stomach then clenched it into a fist. Though she knew many women went on to have babies after being diagnosed with MS, Lily didn't think that was a path she could take. It wasn't the pregnancy that concerned her. In fact, it seemed that being pregnant actually reduced the number of relapses. But what if she couldn't take care of a child the way it needed? What if the child ended up needing to care for her?

"Lily?" Nate's voice pulled her back from her dour thoughts. "Will mentioned the other day that you might be looking for a car."

A car? Right then, Lily wasn't sure she was capable of driving. Even though she'd had every intention of driving when she'd arrived back, she wasn't as confident anymore. If she recovered enough to be physically what she'd been like in London, she'd consider it more seriously. She just hoped that she didn't need to make any trips into Minneapolis any time soon, because she was going to have to prevail upon someone to take her if she couldn't drive.

"I had thought about it. Not sure now," Lily admitted.

Nate nodded. "Well, let me know if you decide to. I have some contacts at the dealerships around here. I can keep an eye out for something."

Lily wanted to protest that she could take care of it herself, but Nate was a car man. It would be stupid to refuse his help just because. "Thank you. I was thinking something along the lines of a smaller SUV. I want something good for winter driving, but that's not too difficult to get in and out of."

"So no monster trucks?"

Lily felt a smile lift the corners of her lips before she could stop it. "Yeah. Gonna have to say no to the monster trucks."

"I'll see if anything comes up and will let you know."

Gripping her purse, Lily stood. "I think I'm going to call it a day. See you tomorrow."

"Good night. Sleep well." Nate's words followed her as she left the library.

Too tired to do anything but undress and brush her teeth, Lily crawled into her bed. Knowing she didn't even have the energy to lift her Bible, she spent time in prayer and then began to recite the verses she'd memorized until sleep finally claimed her.

"Lily?" She felt a touch on her shoulder. "Lily?"

Rolling to her back, Lily suppressed a groan. "What's wrong?"

Cami was sitting at the edge of her bed. "That's what I'm checking on."

Lily lifted an arm and covered her eyes. "Why?"

"It's almost noon."

She lowered her arm and peered at Cami. "Really? Noon?" The sudden pressure of her bladder made her realize that Cami was likely telling the truth. She held a hand out to her sister. "Help me up?"

Cami quickly grasped her hand and pulled her to a sitting position. "Are you...okay?"

"I won't be if I don't get to the bathroom," Lily said, giving her a quick grin. "Be right back."

Surprised that her legs didn't give out beneath her, Lily made her way to the bathroom and then back to the bed a few minutes later. As she sat down next to Cami, she spotted a tray on the nightstand.

"I didn't know if you were planning to get up today, so I brought you something to eat."

"Honestly, I think it may do me well to spend the day in bed. But I am starving."

"Well, why don't you eat a bit and then lie back down again. There's nothing pressing going on today."

Lily settled back against her pillows and reached for the plate with a sandwich on it. "I really should try and do a little more work on Nate's stuff."

"Good luck with that," Cami said. "He took the laptop with him."

After swallowing her first bite, Lily frowned at Cami. "He took it?" Why would he need the laptop?

Cami smiled. "I think he took it so you wouldn't work. Although he didn't actually come out and say that."

Lily fought the urge to be upset with him, but then let it go. "Oh well. His loss."

"There really is nothing going on around here. Lance is at the hospital with Jessa. She will likely come home later today or tomorrow. Baby is doing good. Jessa is nursing as well as pumping. He's struggling a bit with his latch, but drinking well from a bottle so we're hoping for weight gain soon."

She was thankful to hear the good news about the baby. "I'm sure it will be very hard for Jessa to leave him at the hospital."

"Yes," Cami agreed. "But hopefully it won't be for too long."

Cami stayed in the room, chatting with her until she'd finished eating. Though a part of her felt guilty for staying in bed, Lily knew if she wanted to get over the struggles of the past few days, she had to give her body the reprieve it needed.

"I think we're planning on a barbecue for dinner if you feel up to being outside. It's been a nice day. Warm, but not too hot."

Lily nodded. "I'll try to get up for that."

"If not, no problem. Take all the rest you need."

Once alone in the room, Lily got up again and went to take her medication. She really needed to make an appointment with the doctor who had originally diagnosed her. Though she was set for medication for the next month or so, after the past couple of days, it was a clear reminder that she needed to have her health care team in place.

❦

Nate fought the frustration that dogged his steps as he

walked into the manor. He'd spent most the day in Sanford. First talking with the police and fire inspector there then meeting with his employees. He'd taken them all out for a late lunch and had to break the news to them that he wouldn't be rebuilding. It had been a difficult decision, but in the end he knew it was the right one.

The decision to expand had been his dad's. And though he knew that his dad would have rebuilt in a heartbeat, Nate's heart wasn't in it. He was content to just focus on the garage in Collingsworth. Besides, even if he did rebuild, he would have had to hire all new staff. The guys wouldn't be able to wait around for him to be able to pay them. After the meal, he'd given them each a bonus check. It hadn't been much, but he hoped that it would help them in some way.

But even though he knew it had been the right thing to do, it still weighed heavily on him. He wished he could just go back to working on cars. It was what he enjoyed the most. The administration side of things sucked the life out of him sometimes.

"Hey there, Nate."

Nate turned to see Will walking out of the kitchen toward him. "Hey, Will."

"Did you have supper?"

"Not yet." He supposed he should have stopped for something when he'd come through Collingsworth, but he wasn't really hungry.

"Well, come out back. We had a barbecue, and there's plenty of food left."

Nate wasn't sure he would be good company, but the thought of seeing Lily was enticing. "Okay. Just let me put this in the library." He took the laptop bag and set it on the desk before heading out the back door.

The shrieks of the children greeted him as he stepped onto the porch. The idyllic scene set off conflicting emotions within him. Though he was drawn to it, Nate finally accepted that he had no place there. He appreciated the effort the family made to include him, but he knew that he needed to move on soon. Having made the decision about the garage in Sanford, Nate knew he needed to make a few other ones, too.

He spotted Lily right away. She was reclined on a chaise lounge, legs bent with her bare feet planted on the cushion. Laurel's Rose was seated in a chair next to her, and they appeared to be in deep discussion. She didn't look his way, but he didn't know if that was because she was ignoring him or because she didn't know he was there.

❧ Chapter Thirteen ☙

HERE you go," Will said as he handed him a plate. "Fill 'er up."

"Thanks." Nate approached the table where the food was and helped himself to the potato salad and barbecued chicken. As he turned to find a place to sit, he saw that Lily was watching him. He gave her a quick smile before heading to the empty seat next to Will.

After bowing his head to say a prayer for his food, Nate turned to Will. "I'm wondering if you happen to have an empty apartment in that building of yours."

Will's brows rose. "You looking to rent a place? Or is it for someone else?"

"It's for me." Nate took a bite of the potato salad. "It looks like it's going to be a little bit before my house can be rebuilt, so I think I may just rent through the winter and tackle that in the spring."

Will didn't answer right away, and Nate didn't miss the way his gaze went in Lily's direction. "Well, I do have one place coming up. They just gave their notice last week. It's one of the studios though. Not much room."

"That's fine for me. It's not like I have much at the moment."

"Are you sure you wouldn't rather stay here at the manor?" Cami asked. "I'm sure Jessa and Lance wouldn't have a problem with that."

"Today is my day for making decisions," Nate said. "I decided to not rebuild the garage in Sanford, and now I think I need to get a place of my own. It would be for the best. I do appreciate your generosity though. Being able to stay here in the meantime has been a real blessing."

As Will asked the details of what the officials had told him in Sanford, Nate found himself relaxing. Focusing forward was what he needed to do. And though he hadn't given up hoping for a future with Lily, he knew he couldn't live at the manor indefinitely hoping she'd change her mind.

Once he was finished eating, he helped them clean up.

"Ice cream cones," Laurel called out to the kids as she set the ingredients down on the picnic table.

Nate watched the kids gather around the table, clamoring for their dessert. An ache grew in his stomach. One or more of his and Lily's children should have been joining them.

"You're not moving out because I'm here, are you?"

Nate turned to see Lily standing next to him. Her auburn hair was pulled back in a high ponytail and lay over one of her shoulders. For the first time since her arrival, she looked more rested. He also noticed that she seemed more steady on her feet than she had the day before.

Pondering her question, he debated what to tell her. "Partly. This is your home, not mine. If I had known you were on your way back when Lance offered me the place to stay, I would have turned it down. My being here with you is no easier for me than it is for you." She blinked at his comment, and her brows drew together, but she didn't say anything. "Plus, it looks like I will be out of a home for a little longer than a few weeks, so I'd rather have my own place until the house is rebuilt."

"I'm sorry that it's not going to work to rebuild the garage in Sanford."

"Me, too. Mainly because I feel like I'm killing my dad's dream. But that's just what it was. My dad's dream, not mine. It was a lot of stress for me to juggle the two places on my own. I will be happy to just be able to concentrate on the one here."

"I'm sorry if my coming back has complicated things for you." Lily's head dipped. "On top of everything else you've been dealing with."

"Make no mistake, Lily. You coming back would have complicated things for me regardless of what else was going on in my life."

Her gaze jerked up to meet his and for just a brief second, Nate saw a flash of emotion in her eyes. *Good.* She needed to know that while she may have been able to move on, there were still things unresolved for him.

"Maybe I should have just stayed away," she said with a lift of her chin. Nate didn't miss the defensive tone in her voice.

"Maybe you shouldn't have left in the first place," he replied. "It wasn't fair to your family. And it wasn't fair to me."

Anger flashed across her face. Nate's heart clenched at the sight. Though it was cliché, Lily was most beautiful when she allowed her emotions full rein. Happiness, sadness and even anger brought her already vibrant appearance to life.

"The MS diagnosis wasn't fair to me," she said, her voice low. "All I wanted to do was find a way to live with this disease. And I did. You got to go on with your life as normal. You had your job. You got a girlfriend."

Nate saw the flush rise in Lily's face. So it *did* bother her that he'd gone on to date someone else. "Was I supposed to be waiting around for something? I had no idea why you left. For all I knew, you ran off with some British dude. To be honest, I almost wish you had."

Lily's eyes widened. "Seriously?"

"Do you think it's been easy to hear that you left because you'd discovered you had MS? I wish you weren't sick even if it meant you had left to be with someone else."

"Well, wishing isn't going to change anything." She crossed her arms in front of her. "I didn't come back here to complicate your life. I honestly thought you'd moved on. From what Violet said when I got here, it sounded like you had."

"So you felt it was safe being back here because I was dating Crystal?"

"I just thought it would be...easier."

"And then you found out I was staying here at the manor." Rather than answer, Lily just shrugged, her gaze going past him. "Well then, Lily-belle, my moving out should make you happy."

At the use of her nickname, her gaze came back to his for a split second. And for the second time during their conversation he saw a flash of emotion. And it gave him a little more hope. Surely if everything she felt for him was dead, they wouldn't even be having this conversation, let alone it making her mad.

"It doesn't make me happy," Lily said. "Nothing about any of this has ever made me happy."

Nate took a step toward her. "You had to know that if you had told me about the diagnosis, I would have been there for you. Would have done everything I could. I wouldn't have abandoned you."

Lily gave him a sad smile. "Yeah, I know. But I couldn't tell you."

"Couldn't?" Nate asked. "Or wouldn't?"

Her green eyes seemed to liquefy as he stared at her, but no tears flowed. She blinked once then said, "I couldn't."

The faint flickering of hope he'd had earlier sputtered, nearly going out completely. But he couldn't give up on her. On them.

He wouldn't.

∽◦≪

Turning and walking away from Nate this time was almost as hard as it had been the day she'd ended their engagement. But Lily knew she had to do it...and keep doing it. Even though him saying that he would have done everything for her tugged so strongly at her heart, it was also the very thing that kept her from him. This disease had already altered and consumed her life, she didn't want it to do the same for him. After all he'd dealt with, he deserved not to have to bear the burden of what was to come for her.

She didn't have to look around to know that her siblings were watching her walk away from Nate. They'd no doubt been watching—and maybe even listening to—her talk to him. It hadn't been the best place to have the conversation. In fact, she hadn't really thought it through to the end. If she had, she never would have approached him in such a public place.

Not sure where exactly she was going, Lily climbed the porch steps and opened the back door. Inside the kitchen, she paused. After spending all day in her room, she wasn't exactly keen to go back, but she didn't really want to have any type of conversation with her sisters just then either. Not that her going to her room would keep them from seeking her out.

Oh, how she wished she could still handle a long hot bath, but since the heat was no longer her friend, that particular escape was out as well. She had no car to go anywhere. And walking any distance was a risk after just finally feeling steadier on her feet after the past couple of days.

Feeling trapped, Lily let out a long sigh and headed for the stairs. Once in her room, she pulled out her phone and called Megan. It had been a few days since they'd last talked, but she knew her friend would understand.

"Can you come pick me up, Meg?" Lily asked when her friend answered. "I desperately need to get away for a bit."

"Sure. Just dropping something off at my mom's. I'll be there in about twenty minutes."

True to her word, Megan pulled up right on time. Lily had come down to wait on the front steps for her. Thankfully no one had sought her out once she'd gone upstairs. She had a feeling it had been hard for them not to, but she was grateful they'd kept their distance.

"So anywhere particular you want to go?" Megan asked as she turned the car toward Collingsworth.

"Ice cream. I want some ice cream." Lily leaned back in the seat. "They had some for dessert, but I want soft ice cream. Preferably crammed with bits of chocolate."

"Dairy Queen it is," Megan said with a grin.

The tension began to ease from Lily's body as her friend chatted about her day. Megan was the one person who seemed to truly understand how she wanted—needed—to be treated. Though she, too, had gone through a learning curve early on. It gave Lily hope that eventually the rest of her family would get to this point as well.

They ended up hanging out at the ice cream parlor until it closed. Though Lily wasn't excited to get home, she also knew that she didn't want to push herself so soon after the bad day she'd had yesterday. The manor was quiet when Megan dropped her off. Lights were still on, but no one was around downstairs. Lily made her way to her bedroom and slipped inside.

Once again taking advantage of still having a bit of energy left, she showered and then climbed into bed to have her devotions. After reviewing her verse and then praying, Lily found she still wasn't able to fall asleep. She lay curled on her side, staring out the window and allowed herself to relive the earlier conversation with Nate.

It had been easy to not think about it while out with Megan, but now it all came back. She hadn't expected Nate to push her about their breakup. It had actually surprised her. During their relationship, he'd seemed to go out of his way to never argue with her. It seemed that over the past three years, Nate had become more aggressive in how he dealt with things.

Unfortunately, no matter how aggressive he got, it wouldn't change things with Lily. She was fairly certain that if she opened the door to rekindling their romance, he'd be through it in a flash. But she just couldn't do that to him. He hadn't seen the people in the support group she'd gone to in London. The ones who were further along in their fight with MS. Some had to use canes to walk. Others couldn't walk at all. A few couldn't even communicate very well. It had been a sobering reality of what lay ahead for her. Particularly because a few of them hadn't been that much older than her.

She couldn't place that burden on Nate.

This isn't about Nate. You're scared.

Lily let out a sharp breath. No, this was about her not wanting Nate to have to bear the burden of caring for her when her condition worsened. She didn't want her children to be in that position either.

No, this is about you not wanting to take the chance that Nate will abandon you when it gets rough.

He'd said he wouldn't abandon her, and Lily believed him. She knew he had watched his father care for his mother until their death. Nate would be there for her just as his father had been there for his mother. He would care for her. But he shouldn't have to.

You are scared that he might not love you enough to stay. Or that he'll stay with you out of obligation, not love. You are scared.

"Shut up!" Lily hissed in the darkness. This wasn't the first time the voice in her head had tried to make her admit this. But she wasn't scared. She truly was doing this for Nate's sake. He didn't know enough to make the right decision. She did.

Now if she could just get Nate to see that.

✺

The next week settled into an easy rhythm for Lily. She was getting enough sleep. Eating good food. And her body responded well to the schedule. By Friday, Lily was feeling the best she had since leaving London. The family had also gotten to the point where they didn't seem to be constantly on edge about her physical condition.

This weekend promised to hold a range of emotions for her though. Baby Daniel was supposed to be coming home on Saturday after spending just over a week in the hospital. From all reports, he was doing well. Nursing like a champ. Gaining weight and having no further complications that required him to stay longer. Jessa was walking on air.

Unfortunately, come Monday, Cami, Josh and their girls were going to be pulling out and heading back to their home in Tennessee. Strangely enough, though Lily had been fine on her own the last three years, now that she was back home, she found it difficult to think of them not all being together. Cami had been her rock the past week. It would be hard to say goodbye to them on Monday.

Though Nate had been around, he hadn't sought her out. Maybe their conversation a week ago had finally gotten through to him. Lily had continued to work on the bookkeeping for his business, but he hadn't spent much time with her except to answer any questions she might have.

"Hey, Lily."

Looking up from the laptop, Lily saw Jessa walking toward her. "Hey. How's it going?"

"Going good. We're on our way up to the hospital to see

the little guy. Everything going okay here?"

Lily nodded. "I should be finished with this today. Then it will just need Nate to keep up to date with it all."

"Do you think you'll continue to do it for him?" Jessa asked.

"Not sure. I know I need to find something to do. I didn't come back to just sit around."

"I'm sure Nate appreciates your help with all this. It's been a difficult time for him."

Lily stared at Jessa, wondering where she was going with this. "Yes, I'm sure that's true."

Jessa shifted her weight. "Lance said they are going to be tearing down Nate's house today."

And there it was. "I didn't know that."

"Though he's not rebuilding until spring, they need to get rid of the old structure for safety reasons."

Lily's thoughts went back to the time she'd spent there with Nate. It had been his family home. He'd never lived anywhere else. No doubt the majority of the memories of his mom and dad were of them together in their home. A good chunk of her memories with him were also tied to the house.

Feeling tears prick at her eyes, Lily dropped her gaze to the laptop. It was no longer her place to offer comfort to Nate, but the reality was—whether she liked it or not—that man still held a huge part of her heart. Right then, all she wanted to do was go and be by his side while he faced this difficult moment in his life. But she had given up that right three years ago.

"Thanks for letting me know," Lily said as she looked up at her sister. "I'll be praying for him."

Jessa hesitated before nodding. "I thought you should know. Anyway, I'm heading to the hospital. See you later."

Alone in the library, Lily fought the urge to go to Nate's house—no doubt that's where he was—to offer her support.

She couldn't take the chance of him misreading her actions, though. A battle raged within her. Torn between keeping her distance and offering him support. She was also dealing with her own emotional reaction to the destruction of his home. It was a place of significance to their relationship, but now it was gone. Just like things between them.

❧ *Chapter Fourteen* ❧

NATE stood, hands on hips, watching as a large yellow machine broke down the blackened structure that had once been his home. He fought to keep anger at the forefront of his emotions. Anger at the punks who had done this to his home. He needed it to be anger, because if that slipped away there would be sorrow and heartbreak. Those were emotions he didn't want to deal with. At least not in public.

But as he watched, the memories wouldn't leave him alone. Before his mom had gotten sick, the home had been filled with laughter and joy. Even after her diagnosis, she'd tried to keep up the traditions they'd created for their small family. He remembered bringing Lily home to meet his mom. Then over the course of the next seven years they'd spent so much time at the house. Eating dinner with his folks. Sitting around the fire in the backyard roasting marshmallows. Watching movies. They'd sat on that old couch, his arm around Lily, her head resting on his chest. He'd kissed her for the first time as they'd been watching a movie in that basement. And there had been many more kisses over the years.

The burnt-out structure of his home resembled the burnt-out remnants of his relationship with Lily. Maybe it was time to tear that all down, too. Tear it down, clear it out, make room for something new. Maybe if he'd done that sooner, his relationship with Crystal wouldn't have crashed and burned.

"Nate?"

Over the noise of the machines, Nate wasn't sure he'd actually heard her voice say his name. Turning, he couldn't believe it when he saw Lily. Why was she there? He looked past her to see Amy standing with Will next to his truck. Why had they brought her? Surely Will would have known how difficult this would be for him.

Without saying anything, Nate turned back to the growing pile of rubble. He hoped that she'd leave. If she hadn't dashed his hopes so solidly a week ago, he might have taken her appearance as a good sign. He didn't know why she was there, but it certainly wasn't for the reasons he hoped. Of that, he was certain.

Though she didn't say anything more, Nate glanced down to see her still standing at his side, her gaze on the machines diligently working to tear his home down. Suddenly the machine shut down, and silence echoed in its wake.

"Nate, I'm sorry," Lily said, this time her words more audible without the background noise.

He crossed his arms over his chest and stared straight ahead. "You shouldn't be here."

"I just thought--"

"I don't want you here." Barely holding onto his emotions, Nate couldn't look at her. "You can't have it both ways, Lily. Either you're there for me all the way or not at all. I'm not at the place where I can handle you being a friend and nothing more."

"Nate..."

"If you're here as a friend, please just leave. I'd rather deal with this on my own."

Out of the corner of his eye, he saw her take a couple of

steps back then turn around. Clenching his jaw tight, Nate worked to keep his gaze focused forward. He had had to watch her walk away from him one too many times already. Today was not the day he wanted to see that again. He didn't mean to hurt her, but right then he was hurting too much to have to deal with her, too.

He lifted a hand to shield his eyes when he saw someone walking toward him from the site. As the man drew close, Nate recognized Matt.

"Everything going okay?" he asked as Matt came to stand next to him.

"Yep. Structure is down. Now we're just going to start hauling it all away." Matt clapped him on the shoulder. "So sorry about this, man."

Nate nodded. "Must be done."

"Yes, but I'm sure it hasn't been easy to see." Matt's gaze went past him, a frown briefly crossing his face. "Hey, Crystal."

Crystal? Nate swung around to see her a few feet away. Could this day get any worse?

"Talk to you in a bit," Matt said as he gave Crystal a smile and walked past her to where Will's truck was still parked.

"Hi," Crystal said as she stepped to his side. She wrapped her arms around his waist and gave him a quick hug before stepping back. "I was on my way home for lunch when I saw the machines." She looked toward the work area. "I am so sorry to see that. Are you doing okay?"

Looking down at her, Nate wished he had been able to make it work, but he couldn't force his heart to feel something it didn't. "I'm doing okay. I will be glad to get it all over with. This is the hardest part."

"I'm sure. Are you going to rebuild?"

"Eventually. Probably in the spring."

"Are you going to stay at the manor in the meantime?"

Nate looked down at her, trying to read the expression on her face. "Only until I can move into an apartment."

She gave a nod. "How is Lily?"

"Do you really want to talk about Lily, Crys?"

A smile crossed her face. "Honestly, I do. It wasn't until I ended things with you that I realized we really weren't meant to be together. I actually felt kind of relieved. And I'm sure you did, too."

"You're such a sweetheart, I actually wish it could have worked between us. But yes, you're right. I don't think we were meant to be."

"I'd still like to be your friend. That's why I'm here today."

Funny, Nate thought. Two ex-girlfriends offering friendship. He was much more willing to settle into that type of relationship with Crystal than he was with Lily. Maybe that would change in time, but friendship was just so far from his mind whenever Lily was around.

As the machines roared to life again, Crystal tugged on his arm. He bent his head down and heard her say, "I'm going to head back to work. Call me if you need anything. Even just to talk."

Nate leaned down. "Thanks. I appreciate you stopping by."

She gave him a quick wave and headed away. Nate turned back to the job site in time to see the first scoop of the remnants of his house get dropped into a dump truck. He realized then it wasn't just the sentimental things he had lost. He was going to need all those practical things that had gone up in flames as well. A bed. A couch. A television. The important things...

৩৫৩

Well, that had been a colossal mistake.

Lily knew the heavy silence in the truck was because neither Will nor Amy knew what to say. And to be honest, she didn't know either. If Matt hadn't come over to talk to Will, she would not have had to witness the exchange between Nate and Crystal. Not only had she not been sent away, she'd gotten a hug and conversation. Crystal was an ex-girlfriend that Nate seemed willing to be friends with.

Why wouldn't he even consider that with her?

"You okay?" She met Will's gaze in the rear view mirror.

This time Lily knew Will wasn't asking about her physical state. "I shouldn't have gone. It's just...I had memories of that home, too, and it was hard for me to think about losing those. I imagined how much harder it was for him. Just because I don't want a relationship with him doesn't mean I don't care about him."

Amy turned around to look at her. "Are you sure you don't want a relationship with him? Sorry, if that's a personal question."

"I don't want to burden Nate...or anyone for that matter, with the possibility of having to care for me down the road. He saw his dad do that for his mom. We actually talked about it a few times. He said he admired him for what he'd done for his mom, but that it had also been a huge burden for his dad. How could I ask Nate to turn around and do the same thing?" Lily paused. "Would you ask that of Will?"

Amy's brow furrowed as she glanced at the man seated next to her. "I don't know."

"Wouldn't you think that Will deserved a life that didn't include the high possibility of having to care for you later on in your life?"

"I suppose."

"But I would be willing to do that for her, Lil. I love her," Will said. "I would rather live my life with her knowing that was a possibility than to live forever without her."

Amy reached out and laid a hand on his arm. "I know that if the roles were reversed, I would want Will to trust me. To trust my love for him enough to commit to me. Maybe you need to trust that Nate knows—especially given his past—what he wants when it comes to a relationship with you. Of all of us, he would know the true scope of caring for someone. Yet it seems he still wants to do that for you."

Chewing on a fingernail, Lily stared out the window at the houses they passed on the way back to the manor. What if it had been Nate that had been diagnosed with this disease? How would she have felt if he'd broken things off with her without an explanation? She'd been so convinced she was doing the right thing that she'd never considered it from his perspective.

Maybe it was fear. Maybe she *was* scared that at some point down the road as she got worse, he was going to walk out on her. That it would be too much for him, and he'd just leave her. Either way she would end up without him in her life, but at least this way it was her choice.

Lily felt a touch on her arm and looked away from the window to see Amy's hand resting there.

"I know it's hard to trust that someone's love for you will be strong enough to give you what you need from them." She glanced at Will. "That's how it was for me with Will. I wanted everything to be perfect, the way I had dreamed it would be. It didn't work out that way at first. Then I prayed and expected that God would just miraculously fix everything for us. It didn't work out *that* way either. In the end, I had to take a step of faith. In God and in Will. I had to trust that God would do His work in us if I would just let Him. I also had to trust Will when he said he loved me no matter what and that he would be there for me when I needed him.

"I know that Will might let me down at times, but I also know it's not because he doesn't love me. It's because he's human and that's what we humans do. It's easy to commit to someone when the future ahead looks bright and rosy, even though the day after the wedding all that could change. You and Nate have the opportunity to make that decision to commit already knowing that there may be rough waters in the future."

Lily nodded. She knew Amy was right. If she'd received the diagnosis after they were married, she wouldn't have run off and left him. They would have faced it head on. He might still have left her, but her expectation would have been that he'd stick with her. Having it happen before that commitment of their wedding vows had given her an out, and she'd taken it.

Back at the manor, Lily retreated to her room to think over what Amy had said. Though she was older than her by a few years, Amy had shown more maturity in her relationship with Will than she had so far with Nate.

Sitting on the edge of her bed, Lily reached for her Bible. She unzipped the cover and found the note card she'd written out the night before. Though the verse from Proverbs was one she'd learned in Sunday school years ago, it was the one verse that had stood out to her the night before as she read her devotions.

Trust in the Lord with all your heart, and lean not on your own understanding; in all your ways acknowledge Him, and He shall direct your paths.

Clutching the card in her hand, Lily knew that though she had said she trusted the Lord, she hadn't really. And she certainly had been leaning on her own understanding. In her mind, with all she knew about how MS progressed, she'd decided already that it would be too much for Nate. When she'd made her decision it hadn't been after spending much time in prayer over it. She hadn't sought God's will for her and Nate. In fact, she'd been quite angry with Him when she'd first been diagnosed.

Why couldn't she trust God and Nate fully with this part of her life? Lily looked down at the card she held, rubbing her thumb along its smooth surface. She knew why. She'd always known why, but she'd hesitated to face it since things seemed to be going so well. But the feelings were all still there.

Her mother had abandoned her. Though Elizabeth had essentially abandoned *all* of them when she'd decided she couldn't raise them and turned them over to her mother, it still hurt Lily that *she* hadn't been good enough for her to keep.

Gran had handed her off to Jessa. At a time when she'd needed a mother to help her navigate the rough waters between being a pre-teen and a woman, Gran had begun to take less and less interest in her life. And while on one hand it had been nice to not have someone keeping tabs on her twenty-four seven, it had left Lily feeling like she'd been too much hassle for the older woman. Jessa had tried to be there for her, but she had had her own struggles as she'd been going to school and trying to keep things going around the manor.

And when Jessa and Lance had gotten together, Lily had felt as if she'd been cut loose. She was eighteen then, an adult by some definitions, and yet still needing the guidance of...someone. By then she'd become involved with Nate. Even now she wondered if part of what had drawn her to him had been him being older than her. He'd seemed so stable with his job at his dad's garage and so much more mature than the guys her age. And of course it hadn't hurt that she found him terribly handsome.

Now, however, she looked at him and saw strength. An inner strength that had only been there in small amounts ten years ago. Much of what had happened to him over the past few years would have broken a lesser man. She should have trusted him to have the strength to deal with what her future now involved.

Unfortunately, after their exchange at his house today, Lily saw that she'd come to her realizations a little too late.

৩৩৯

Nate spent the next week leaving the manor early and getting home late. He hadn't been interested in any more run-ins with Lily. Each one seemed to leave him more confused and hurt than the last. She'd made her decision, and it was time he accepted that and moved forward.

Thankfully the office had been repaired early in the week so he'd had somewhere to go to work. Will had also let him know that he could move into the studio apartment the next week. He would need to go shopping for a bit of furniture before then.

His cell phone rang, dragging his thoughts from the plans he'd been making. He leaned back in his new office chair as he picked it up, pausing when he saw the name on the screen.

Lily.

After a brief hesitation, he tapped the screen to answer it. "Proctor." Even as he said his name, he knew it was ridiculous. Lily had phoned his cell. She would know that he'd seen who was calling before answering.

There was a brief pause. "Hi, Nate. It's Lily."

Her voice washed over him. The nearly-three years he'd gone without hearing her voice hadn't seemed as long as the past week. "Lily. What can I do for you?"

"I was just wondering if your offer was still open."

Nate leaned forward, bracing his elbow on the new desk he'd had delivered that week. "What offer was that?"

"Helping me find a new car."

Oh, that offer. Nate let out a silent breath. There was just no way he could go hang with her for several hours and not walk away with more hurt. "Sure, I can do that. I'll give Rod over at Midtown Auto Sales a call and let him know to expect you. He will help you out and give you the best deal he can. Just tell him I sent you."

There was another stretch of silence, this one a little longer than the last.

"Okay. Thank you for your help." Her voice was soft and low. "I appreciate it. I'm sorry for bothering you at work."

Before he could say anything more, the call ended. A sick feeling sat in his gut. In that moment he realized this was the very reason she'd ended things with him. When she called and asked for his help, he'd turned her away. He'd let her down. Even after he'd told her that he'd be there to help with this, he'd left her to deal with it alone.

She'd done so much for him since she'd returned and had only asked for help this one time. He was no kind of man that deserved someone like her. He called himself a few choice names. *Jerk* being at the top of his list. So what if it caused him some pain to help her out? If he was any type of man, he would buck up and deal with it.

Nate pressed the screen of his phone to call her back. It rang several times before she answered.

"I'm sorry." He knew she knew it was him. That was undoubtedly why it had taken her so long to answer.

"It's okay. I understand you're busy."

"No, it wasn't that." Nate rubbed his forehead. "When were you thinking of going?"

"Please don't worry about it, Nate. I shouldn't have presumed. I trust that your friend will help me out."

"Lily." Nate said her name through clenched teeth. "When were you thinking of going?"

Silence.

"Lily, just tell me when you want to go."

"My schedule is pretty wide open. I thought whenever it was convenient for you."

"Meet me at Midtown in an hour."

"An hour?"

"Yes. Is that a problem?" Nate just wanted to get this over with.

"No. No. I'll be there."

"Okay. See you then."

After ending the call, Nate pushed back from his desk and

shoved a hand through his hair. He knew he was doing the right thing, but the knot in his stomach made it difficult for him to appreciate that fact.

❧ Chapter Fifteen ❧

LILY set her phone down on the bed and took a deep breath. Having realized several days ago that Nate was avoiding her, she hadn't known how else to get hold of him. She had thought about just waiting up for him one night to try to talk to him. But something still held her back.

Three years was a long time to be apart, and she knew that they had both changed. She was no longer the young girl who had relied on him for so much. Even her wanting to get a car was a sign of how she'd changed. Back then, he'd driven her most places she'd needed to go. She'd just arranged her life around when he was available to take her. If she did have to go somewhere when he hadn't been available, she'd driven Gran's old car or borrowed Jessa's. She hadn't even bothered to buy a car even though she could have afforded one.

He had been her world, but three years without him had taught her to fend for herself and to grow up.

Nate had always been reserved. Most of the girlfriends Lily had back then teased her about picking the boring boy to date. None had realized that to her, he was anything but. When it was just the two of them or if they were with his parents, they'd had fun. They liked the same kind of movies and television shows. They'd loved to watch B-movies and see who could figure out the plot twists before they happened. Or watch horror movies and try to guess the order people were going to stupidly die.

She'd love the times they'd sat around the fire pit in his parents' backyard roasting marshmallows. Nate had always done hers, taking the time to make sure it was roasted to golden perfection before making her a s'more. Though she knew she wasn't high on his priority list, when he did have time, he was there focused on her. It was those moments that had kept her with him, hoping that in years to come, they would become the norm rather than the exception.

Lily had loved that though Nate rarely smiled around others, when he saw her, he always had. Their gazes could meet across a distance and he would always...always...smile at her. Even if it was just a quick lift of one corner of his mouth.

Ending things with him had devastated her because she knew that no one else would ever know her heart the way he did. They'd had a connection she wouldn't—and didn't want—to share with any other man. But before she could be completely at peace about asking for a second chance, Lily needed to know that he knew what she did about her diagnosis and made any decision with that knowledge.

She pushed to her feet, wishing she had the time to redo her hair and make-up, but she was lucky she had enough time to change. Knowing the day was warm, Lily chose an outfit that would keep her cool. She settled on a turquoise sleeveless shirtwaist dress with a slightly flared skirt.

After smoothing her hair with her brush, Lily sat on the edge of the bed to put her shoes on. She'd chosen a pair of white gladiator-style sandals that fit tightly to her feet and ankles. Gone were the days of loose fitting sandals or even flip-flops for any place but home. Any shoe she wore now had to fit securely in case she didn't lift her foot enough.

She picked up a bottle of perfume from the nightstand

and dabbed a little on her wrists. It was the same scent she'd worn for years. It had also been Nate's favorite. She had no idea what he would think of the subtle—or perhaps not so subtle—way she was acknowledging their past.

Lily went to the open door of Jessa and Lance's suite and peeked in. "Hey, Jessa, can I borrow your car?"

Jessa looked up from where she was nursing the baby. "My car? Sure." She tilted her head. "You look very pretty. What's the occasion?"

Lily took a quick breath. "I'm meeting Nate to look at cars."

Her sister's eyes widened. "Do you think that's such a good idea?"

"I need to get us back to at least being friends before I can ask more of him."

A small smile curved Jessa's lips. "You think you might get back together?"

Lily shrugged. "I'm not sure if I've left it too late with him. We'll see."

"I'll be praying for both of you." She gave her a wider smile. "My keys are on the hook in the kitchen."

Lily walked to where Jessa sat, pressed a kiss to her cheek and gently touched the baby's head. "See you later."

﹏

"Think your girl's here," Rod said.

"She's not my girl," Nate ground out before turning to see that indeed, it was Lily headed in their direction. She moved gracefully toward them, her auburn hair glinting in the bright sunlight. Recalling what he'd read about heat affecting those with MS, he hoped the day wouldn't be too much for her. He hadn't even thought to check the weather to see how hot it would be.

"Hi," Lily said with a smile as she reached them.

"Lily, this is Rod Winters. Rod, this is Lily Collingsworth."

They shook hands and then Rod said, "So Nate mentioned you're looking for a smaller SUV?"

"Yes. A cross-over, I think they call them."

Rod nodded. "We've got a couple of them on the lot you can test drive."

Nate walked beside Lily as Rod headed toward a row of parked cars. For the next fifteen minutes, he listened as Lily asked questions--informed ones--about the vehicles Rod showed her. Nate wasn't even sure why she had wanted him there. In the past, she would have left all of this kind of stuff up to him. In fact, if she'd wanted a car when they were engaged, he would have just bought it and given it to her. She wouldn't have cared about much more than how it looked. Today she was asking about safety records and mileage. Just one more example of how she didn't need him anymore.

"What do you think? Nate?"

Pulling his thoughts back to the matter at hand, Nate focused on Lily. "Rod has done a pretty good job with the pros and cons and answering the questions you had. I think it all comes down to which cons you can live with and which pros you can't."

Her brow furrowed for a second before she nodded. He saw uncertainty cross her face as she clutched the strap of her purse. Maybe this wasn't as easy for her as he'd thought. She had clearly done her homework, but when push came to shove, she still didn't trust her own judgment.

Nate glanced at his friend. "Can you give us a few minutes, Rod?"

"Sure thing, buddy." He jerked his head toward the building. "I'll be inside if you need me."

As the man walked away, Nate turned to Lily. "Let's go sit in my truck and talk about it. It's getting a bit warm."

Lily nodded and walked beside him to the truck. He opened the door for her and watched as she pulled herself up onto the seat. He would have loved to help her, but wasn't about to put himself in the position of being slapped down again.

After getting behind the wheel, he started it up and cranked the air conditioning. It didn't take long for cold air to begin to stream from the vents.

"Okay, so what are you feeling about what Rod showed you? Do any of them interest you or would you rather look at a few other places?"

Lily let out a sigh. "I feel like if I give myself too many options, I'll never be able to make a decision."

Nate nodded. "It sounds like you've done some research though. Out of all that, before talking to Rod, which was the one that appealed to you most?"

Lily told him. "It seemed the safest. And I did actually like how it looked."

"Rod's not a dealer for that line of vehicles, so we'll have to go to another dealership. There's one on the south side of town. I know a guy who works there, too. I'll call to see if they have any in stock for you to test drive."

It didn't take long for him to confirm that they did, so he let them know they'd be there in a few minutes. "Let me just go tell Rod."

"I'm sorry to have wasted his time."

"Don't worry about it. That's the life of a salesman. He understands."

After letting Rod know, Nate headed back, his steps faltering a bit when he saw Lily standing outside the truck.

"I'll just follow you," Lily said as he reached her.

Nate gave a shake of his head. "Get back in the truck. I'll drive you there and then bring you back here."

She hesitated but when Nate opened the door and gave her a determined look, she climbed in without argument.

"Thank you again for helping me," Lily said as he drove the car out onto Main Street.

"Well, I owed you for all the bookkeeping you did for me. I'm happy to be able to return the favor."

"I hope I'm not premature in buying a car, but I saw the doctor this week, and he said I'm fine to drive. I will have to have some testing done before I go to renew my driver's license just to have it on file that I've been medically cleared to drive. And then, from what I've read, I'll have to renew my license every year instead of every four years."

Nate frowned. He hadn't even thought about how she would have to deal with getting a driver's license after being diagnosed with MS. "Well, I hope the tests go well so you are able to put your new car to good use."

Lily nodded. "I need to be able to get to the Twin Cities every once in a while without having to rely on someone taking me."

She should have been able to rely on him. But she'd never given him that chance.

Gripping the steering wheel, Nate tried to keep his thoughts from going in that direction. He was just surprised she was actually talking to him about this kind of stuff. "Do you think you'll have to go there frequently?"

"As long as things stay stable it should only be for the odd scan or trip to a specialist. But if things should start to decline, it could be more often."

"But would you be able to drive then?"

Lily was silent for a moment. "No, probably not."

Nate let the conversation drop as he turned into the lot of the other dealership. Once they'd hooked up with his contact there, Nate let Lily take the lead once again. They had one of the SUVs she was interested in on the lot, so the guy got them set up to take a test drive.

When he handed the keys to Lily, she looked at Nate. "Did you want to drive it?"

"Nope. This is gonna be your ride, so you need to be the one testing it out."

As they got into the vehicle, Nate realized that he'd never been in the passenger seat while Lily drove. In all their years as a couple, if they'd been going anywhere together, he'd always been the one to drive. He could tell she was nervous by the way she bit her lip and gripped the steering wheel with both hands.

He reached over and covered her hand. When she looked at him, her eyes were wide. "Relax. Focus on how it feels to you. Is the seat comfortable? Does the position of the steering wheel feel right? Just imagine you're driving one of the family cars."

Lily nodded, and he lifted his hand from hers. He saw her take a breath and exhale before carefully backing out of the parking spot. "Why don't you head to the highway that goes around the city and we'll come back in on the north end of town."

It took a few minutes, but finally Lily seemed to relax behind the wheel and gain confidence as she guided the vehicle along the highway. Coming back through the city, he could sense again that she was a little nervous with the traffic, but he was sure that had more to do with it not being her vehicle than her driving ability.

Aside from the odd comment about the car or their surroundings, the trip was made in silence. When she finally pulled into the spot in the lot, she leaned back against the seat, dropped her hands into her lap and let out a long sigh.

"Good job," Nate said and gave her a quick smile when she looked his way. "What do you think?"

"I like it." She reached out to grip the wheel. "I think I want to buy it."

Nate was surprised at her quick decision. "You don't want to take a little time to think about it?"

Lily shook her head. "After all my research, I had decided

this was the top of my list and now that I've driven it, I'm convinced it's the right one."

Well, it was her money, so far be it from him to argue with her. Not that he would have. He had to admit the car rode pretty nice for something that wasn't a truck. "Let's go have a chat with the sales guy."

Once inside the office, the salesman approached them, a broad smile on his face. "So? How did it feel?"

"I loved it," Lily said.

The guy's smile grew even wider—if that were possible—no doubt because of the sound of money coming his way. "Well, let's do this."

Nate headed toward a row of seats, prepared to wait while Lily hashed out her deal. She didn't really need him for this part. It wasn't like she had to bargain the guy for the best price. Money was not an object for the Collingsworth family.

"Nate?"

He turned to see Lily looking at him, both her hands once again gripping her purse strap. He motioned to row of chairs by the window. "I'm just going to wait here while you finish up."

"Oh." She glanced at him and then at the sales guy waiting for her just outside the door of the office.

"Did you want me to come, too?" Nate offered, though he really didn't want to be in there with her. Or rather, he did, but for all the wrong reasons.

"Could you? This is all new to me."

With a nod, Nate jammed his hands into his pockets and followed her into the small office. For the next half hour, he listened as Lily conducted her business. It seemed that it had been strictly for moral support that she'd wanted him to come, because she handled it all quite well on her own.

When they finally left, she was the proud owner of a brand new SUV. Because she'd wanted certain additions and a specific color, her vehicle wouldn't be delivered for a couple of weeks. From the look on her face that didn't seem to be a problem.

"I can't believe I just went out and bought a car," she said once they were back in his truck.

"No second thoughts?" Nate asked as he started up the engine.

Lily paused then said. "No. Not about this."

He shot her a glance at that comment. "But you're having second thoughts about something else?"

She didn't look at him or reply right away. He saw she had bent her head and was gripping her purse tightly in her lap. As the silence lengthened, Nate figured she wasn't going to reply. However, when he pulled to a stop behind Jessa's car, she finally spoke.

As he put the truck into park, he glanced over to find her looking at him. "Would you be willing to..." Her brows drew together. "Would you be willing to meet with my doctor?"

Nate turned to face her more fully, his back pressed against the door. "Why?"

"I need you to understand."

"Understand what exactly?"

She looked away from him, her gaze once again dropping to her lap. "My doctor isn't just my doctor. He's also married to a woman who was diagnosed many years ago with MS."

Nate wasn't sure how to take what she was asking of him. "And the purpose of my meeting with him?"

"He can tell you what it's like. Living with a person who has advanced MS."

"Why do I need to know that? You've told me it's over between us."

Lily nodded. "I want you to know what I do about what lies ahead for me."

"You want me to see how hard it is and then thank you for sparing me that?"

Her shoulders lifted and fell. "I don't know. I just feel like maybe having more information, might make it...easier for you."

"I wasn't looking for easy when I decided to marry you, Lily. I was prepared to vow in sickness and health, in the same way my dad had done with my mom. I know that plenty of people never face that sickness part to the degree my dad did, but I also knew it could happen and still I was willing to vow that to you. I don't need to meet with someone to find out how fortunate I was that you ended things so I didn't have to deal with it."

Lily nodded and fumbled for something in her purse. She reached over and opened her door and before Nate could stop her, she'd slid off the seat to stand on the road. Turning, she reached in and laid a card on the console between the seats. "If you change your mind, he is willing to meet with you."

He watched as she walked to Jessa's car and got in. She didn't hesitate to start it up and drive away, leaving Nate sitting there wondering what was going through her mind. Was she really just trying to give him the information to help him understand that she'd made the right decision for both of them? He picked up the card and stared at it.

His first instinct was to crumple it in his fist. Clearly this was the reason she'd asked him to come along today. Not to offer a second chance. Not to spend time with him. No, she had wanted to ease her own guilt by giving him a way to find out for himself that he'd had a lucky break when she'd broken their engagement.

Nate tossed the card into the cup holder in the console and put the truck in gear. He didn't need to talk to the doctor to know what it would have been like years from then with Lily. It just wouldn't have mattered. He would have done what he needed to in order to care for her because he had loved her. But she hadn't trusted him. That was the bottom line. She may say it was about wanting to save him from a life that required him caring for her, but in the end, all it said to him was that she hadn't trusted in their love.

❧ *Chapter Sixteen* ☙

IF Lily had thought things would change after that day with Nate, she had been sorely mistaken. It had been almost three weeks, and she had only seen him from a distance at church. He'd moved out of the manor the week after they'd gone car shopping, and when she'd asked her doctor if he'd called, he had said no.

Sweat slid down her back, soaking the waistband of the shorts she wore. It was way too hot for her to be out here, but she wanted to help Will. He'd approached her to see if she'd give him a hand setting up a surprise dinner for him and Amy. It looked like Will was ready to take a second shot at marriage. She was happy for them. Since she'd returned to the manor, she and Amy had become good friends. Amy was much like Megan in her approach to Lily's MS. Both of them treated her like she didn't have it, but never questioned her if she had to back out of something.

"Maybe you should go back to the manor," Will suggested as he came to where she was hanging a lantern on a tree branch. "It's way hotter today than I thought it was going to be. And you've been out here for hours."

"I want it perfect for you and Amy," Lily told him. "And I'm doing okay."

She had purposely come out early so that she could work slowly. Will had taken Amy and Isabella on a shopping trip to Minneapolis the day before, which had gotten Amy out of the way so they could do most the preparations before they'd gotten back a short time ago. Laurel was in charge of the food. Violet had planned to help with the decorating, but one of her kids had come down with some sort of bug overnight, so she'd had to stay home with her. It had meant some extra work for Lily, but she was happy to do it for them.

"It looks beautiful," Will said as he glanced around. From what he'd told Lily, this clearing held some sort of significance for them.

Lily brushed a bead of sweat from her cheek. "Let me just finish this up and then it's all yours. I think Laurel will be here shortly with the food."

"And you'll bring Amy out here?" Will asked.

"I'm going to try. That girl of yours can be a little inquisitive." Lily smiled. "But I'm going to do my best to make sure she doesn't suspect anything."

"She went into town right after we got back to help Julia pick out something for the baby. Isabella tagged along, so I think we're in the clear for a little while."

After Will had helped her hang the last lantern, they began to light the candles inside each one. White tulle was strung from the branches of the trees, and Will had set up a stereo for some music. The last thing to be decorated was the intimate round table Will had carted out to the clearing. Lily spread a tablecloth over its surface and set a small floral arrangement with candles in the center. All it needed now was the dishes and food.

She heard a commotion and turned to see Laurel and Matt come into the clearing carrying boxes.

"The food has arrived," Laurel said with a grin.

It didn't take long for them to set the table with the dishes Laurel had brought and then place the meals under silver domes.

"It smells heavenly," Lily said. "Is there more at the house?"

Laurel laughed. "You know me too well."

After making sure everything was how Will wanted it, they left him alone in the clearing, pacing around the table. Back at the house, Amy was talking with Jessa when they walked in. She looked at them and then asked, "Where's Will?"

"He said he had to do something. He'll be back in a few minutes." Lily felt her pockets and then frowned. "Oh rats."

"What's wrong?" Amy asked.

"I was out for a walk and think I dropped my phone somewhere." She looked at Amy. "Would you come with me to see if I can find it?"

"Sure." Amy stood up. "Where were you walking?"

"I took that path out past Jessa's greenhouse."

Amy nodded. "That's the one that goes to the clearing where we had Isabella's party. We'd better go before it gets any darker or we won't be able to find it tonight."

Lily allowed Amy to take her hand and pull her toward the back door. She tried to ignore the tingling in her legs and the weakness that was spreading from her lower back downwards. There was no doubt she was going to pay for what she'd done today, but right then she just wanted to get Amy to Will and then she'd deal with it.

"Supper will be ready when you get back," Laurel called after them.

"I heard lots about the party," Lily commented as they walked toward the path. "Will said you did an amazing job planning it."

"It was a ton of fun. Hope I can do another one next year for her."

"So you've made up your mind to move here?" Lily asked.

Amy glanced at her. "I don't know. I want to, but I'm not sure what's in Will's mind about our future just yet. I don't want to rush anything, but I can't just stay on indefinitely at the manor."

"You know that's not a problem," Lily said. "You're always welcome here."

As they drew closer to the clearing, soft music could be heard through the stillness of the early evening air. Amy paused and looked at Lily. "Is that your phone?"

Lily shrugged. "Maybe someone is calling it."

They continued down the path, Amy leading the way. As she came to the clearing, she stopped dead in her tracks. Lily gave Will a thumbs-up and slowly stepped back from the woman who would no doubt soon be her sister-in-law.

"Hey, beautiful."

Lily swallowed hard and blinked away tears as she heard Will greet Amy. Turning, she began to retrace her steps back to the manor. With each step, tears began to fill her eyes. After walking slowly for a couple of minutes with blurred vision, she stumbled over a root and fell to her knees. Grateful that she was a distance from the clearing, Lily leaned forward to brace her hands on the rough ground. Her intent had been to push herself back up to standing, but instead her shoulders hunched forward as she tried to keep her sobs from becoming audible to the couple who were so joyfully moving forward in their life together.

With her gasping breaths loud to her own ears, Lily made the effort to gain control and get to her feet. As she took a step, she knew that she'd done far too much and exposed her body to way too much heat. Added to that was her inability to sleep well over the last three weeks, and she knew she was well on her way to an exacerbation at the very least or quite possibly an attack.

The trembling in her legs made each step more difficult. Lily grabbed on to the surrounding trees, ignoring the pain as small, sharp branches jabbed into her palms. She was determined to make sure Will and Amy wouldn't hear her before calling for help. The last thing she wanted to do was ruin their moment, but she knew getting back to the manor on her own wouldn't be possible at that point.

∽∾

Nate knocked on the front door of the manor, looking around at the cars parked in the driveway. He knew it probably wasn't the smartest thing he'd ever done, but he'd volunteered to deliver Lily's car once it arrived.

Apparently Lily had been in to sign the necessary papers and get it licensed but there had been damage done to it en route so they'd had to take the time to repair it before releasing it to her. He'd been staying away from her once again, but when his buddy at the dealership had let him know that it was ready to go, he'd offered to take it out to the manor. It just seemed fitting after he'd been with her when she'd picked it out. And after a few weeks of keeping his distance, he had to admit, he just plain wanted to see her.

The door swung open to reveal Lance standing in the foyer. "Hey, Nate. How's it going?"

"Not too bad. I just brought Lily's car out for her. Is she here?"

Lance motioned him in. "She should be back in a couple of minutes."

Nate joined them in the kitchen where it looked like they were preparing food. "I don't want to interrupt your supper." He laid the keys on the counter. "If you could just make sure Lily gets these."

"You don't have to rush off," Jessa said as she swayed with her baby in her arms. "She'll be right back."

Nate shifted from one foot to the other. Maybe it was just as well she wasn't there. "I should get back to the garage."

"You planning to walk?" Lance asked.

"No. One of the guys should be on his way to pick me up."

Lance glanced down as his phone rang. He pulled it from his belt and stared at the display. "Lily?" He paused, his brow furrowing as he listened. "What's wrong?"

Nate's heart stuttered to a stop and then started up again at an alarming rate.

"Let's go," Lance motioned to Nate. "Lily needs help."

Without hesitation, Nate followed Lance out the back door and took off at a run in the direction Lance indicated. It seemed to take forever to find her on the path even though he knew it was just minutes.

He spotted her slumped on the ground, her face in her hands. "Lily!"

She glanced up at him, her face ravaged by tears. Immediately she covered her face again. Nate had already scooped her into his arms by the time Lance joined them.

"What's wrong, Lily?" Lance asked.

"Just did too much. Too hot," she said, her head resting on Nate's shoulder.

He wondered if she could hear how hard his heart was pounding. He was scared out of his mind. The fact that she hadn't resisted his efforts to help her spoke more to her physical state than anything else. The others met them on the back porch as Nate climbed the stairs. Jessa opened the door to let them into the kitchen.

Nate set her down on a chair. "Do you need to go to the hospital?"

Lily shook her head. She lifted her hands and rubbed the tears from her cheeks. Nate frowned when he saw the streaks of blood left behind. He reached for her hands and turned them palms up. "What happened?"

"I was trying to grab on to the branches to help me walk."

"Is this a relapse?" Laurel asked as she approached. She handed Nate a damp paper towel, and he gently wiped the blood from Lily's hands.

"I don't think so. These are all the same symptoms that pop up when I get overtired, overheated or overstressed. It's the same thing I had when I first got here. They call it a pseudo-exacerbation. It's old symptoms flaring up. I just need rest."

"Are you sure you don't need to go to the hospital?" Nate asked again.

She looked up at him, her eyes seeming to dominate her face. "No. If I'm not showing improvement by Monday, I'll call my doctor. I have medication I can take. And I just need rest. I'll be fine. Thank you for your help." Her gaze went to her family gathered around them. "Sorry to have worried you. Please don't say anything to Will and Amy about this."

"We won't, but they're going to know something is wrong," Jessa pointed out.

"We'll deal with that tomorrow," Lily said. "Tonight is for them."

Nate glanced at Jessa. "Something going on with Will and Amy?"

"Will's proposing," Lily said. "We helped him get everything ready. I don't want anything to spoil this special time for them."

Nate looked at the streaks of dirt mingled with blood on Lily's face and felt his heart clench. He had never gone to the trouble of setting up a super romantic proposal for Lily. They'd just sort of eased into their engagement. Lily had even helped pick out her own ring. Had she thought he didn't care because he hadn't taken the extra effort to propose like that? Was that one of the reasons she hadn't trusted his love for her?

Laurel moved past him with a cloth and carefully wiped

Lily's face. "You sure you're okay, sweetie?"

Nate saw her smile, but it was small and quick and definitely didn't reach her eyes. "I'm not, but I will be." She looked at Lance. "Can you help me upstairs?"

Though it was like a stab in the heart that she didn't ask him, Nate knew he had no right. He took a step back, away from the intimate group of people gathered around her. These were the ones she turned to. The ones whose love she did trust enough to help her.

He heard a quick notification from his phone. Silently he let himself out the back door. He rounded the house to where his ride waited, suddenly determined to do what he had to to convince Lily she could count on him to be there for her. And step one was to phone her doctor and talk with him. He was pretty sure she wouldn't accept anything from him unless she knew that he had the knowledge of just how difficult it might be in the years to come. All he knew was that seeing her there on the path today had just about killed him. He wanted to be there to help her. This woman still held his heart, whether she wanted to or not, and he wanted to prove himself worthy of holding hers.

He might have kept himself physically away from her for the past couple of weeks, but he'd thought about her every single day. *Every. Single. Day.* To know that she was so close and yet completely out of his reach tortured him. He'd tried to give her the space she clearly wanted from him, but maybe now it was time to try a different tactic. He would do what he could to prove to her that his love was strong and able to handle whatever life threw at them. Now and in the future.

༒

Lily knew she shouldn't have been disappointed when she realized Nate had left. But she'd needed help to get upstairs before Will and Amy came home, and she wasn't sure it was wise to ask for that from Nate. With things the way they were between the two of them, she didn't want to set herself up for any further heartache.

She'd been shocked to hear him say her name and then to look up and find him there with her on the path. Shocked, but oh so glad. Even though she knew what had caused the flare-up. Even though she knew that it was likely nothing that couldn't be healed with some rest and medication. Each time it happened, she couldn't fight that panic and fear that rose within her as she waited for a new symptom to manifest itself. These flare-ups were most serious if a new symptom arose along with the old. So far, that hadn't happened. The worst was always her ability to walk and then some fuzziness in the brain. Those she could handle, but any new symptom would likely mean a worsening of the MS.

"You okay?" Lance asked as he helped her to the edge of her bed. "Do you need Laurel or Jessa to come help you?"

"I'm here." Lily looked past Lance to see Laurel. She came to sit next to her. "Let me know what you need."

"I'm gonna head back downstairs. Text if you need anything," Lance said before leaving the room.

"I was just going to rest for a couple of hours." Lily brushed at the dirt on her knees. "But if you're willing to help me, I think I'd feel better if I had a shower."

"Sure, I can do that."

Over the next thirty minutes, Lily was reminded once again of why she hadn't wanted to burden Nate or her family with her care. But there was no way she could have showered on her own. She could hire someone, but right now the times she needed help to that degree were sporadic. Paying someone to be on-call just didn't make sense. This flare-up was definitely her fault, and she knew the best way to not need help unexpectedly was to take care to not do the things that caused one in the first place. Maybe she just needed to put someone on-call when it appeared her schedule was going to place demands on her more than it usually did.

Unfortunately, life didn't always unfold in the ways planned. Since her return to Collingsworth, she'd learned that in a big way.

"Thanks," Lily said as she sat down on the edge of the bed. "Sorry if I've delayed supper."

"Don't worry about that. Just rest." Laurel helped her to lie down and covered her with a blanket. "You have your phone?"

Lily held it up. "I'll text if I need something, but I think I'm going to sleep til morning."

"Okay. Sleep well." Laurel headed for the door then turned. "By the way, Nate was here to drop off your car."

"Really? It's here?"

"Yep. The keys are on the counter downstairs. You might want to thank him."

Lily stared at the door in the now-darkened room. Yes, she probably should thank him. For more than just the car. Though exhaustion pulled at her, she lifted her phone and debated whether to text or phone him.

After some debate, she found his contact info and tapped the screen to call him.

❧ *Chapter Seventeen* ❧

"**L**ILY," he said when he answered, so different from the last time she'd called. "How are you doing?"

His words washed over her as she curled onto her side, the phone pressed to her ear. She closed her eyes and said, "I'm doing better. Laurel helped me shower and get into bed. With some rest, I should be good as new."

"I'm glad to hear that." There was silence for a moment. "What happened?"

"I just overdid it. The day ended up hotter than I had anticipated."

"So why didn't you stop? Or ask for help?"

"Everyone was busy, and I didn't want to let Will down on his special night. He'd worked hard to plan this out perfectly for Amy. Honestly, as long as she says yes—which I'm sure she will—it will have been worth it."

"Still. You need to be careful." The quiet admonishment in his words warmed her.

"I will be." Exhaustion slowly crept over her, pulling her

towards sleep. She popped her eyes open to keep from drifting off mid-conversation with Nate. "Listen, I also wanted to thank you for bringing my car out."

"You're welcome. The damage is all fixed, and it's ready to go."

Lily sighed. "I guess I won't be driving it for a few days."

"Yeah. Probably better not to."

Silence stretched between them. There were so many words Lily wanted to say. Instead, she said the ones she didn't want to. "I need to get some sleep, so rather than risk falling asleep while I'm talking with you, I'll just say goodnight now."

"Sleep well."

After Lily touched the screen to end the call, she stared at it for a moment then tapped another icon. This time her file of pictures popped up. She found the oldest pictures and tapped the first one. As the image filled the screen, she gazed at it. Happiness radiated from her, and even Nate sported a rare smile. It was the night they'd gotten engaged. Everything lay ahead of them. Marriage. Children. Years of love together. Within eight months, all of that had changed for her.

If she'd had her way, they would have been married by that point, but Nate had kept putting off setting a date because of the work with his dad. And in the end, it had been just as well. If he hadn't had time for a wedding, he certainly didn't have time to spend taking care of her.

Just before she drifted off to sleep, Lily realized she'd forgotten to do her devotions.

Forgive me, Lord.

❧☙

Nate stared at the large house that matched the address he'd been given earlier. As soon as he'd gotten back to the garage, he'd found the card Lily had left in his truck and made the call. What he hadn't expected was for the doctor to tell him to head right over to his house. He'd thought that he'd make an appointment and get to see him sometime in the next week or so. That it happened so quickly was a bit disconcerting, but now that he'd started on this path, he was going to follow it through.

He got out of the truck and followed the brick sidewalk to the front door. It was large with etched glass panels on either side of it. He pressed the doorbell and stepped back to wait. It wasn't long before the door swung open to reveal an older gentleman in pressed slacks and a polo shirt. Nate felt a little underdressed in his jeans and T-shirt but at least they were clean.

"Nate?" the man asked as he held out his hand.

Nate shook it as he nodded.

"I'm Dr. Bennett. Please, come in." The doctor stepped back and motioned for Nate to enter the foyer. "I'm glad you called. Lily wasn't sure that you would."

"It took me a little while to make up my mind."

The doctor gave him a smile. "That's completely understandable."

Nate followed the man into a large well-decorated living room. It wasn't something he'd ever be comfortable living with, but the doctor seemed perfectly at ease as he gestured to a chair and then sat down on the one facing it.

Nate rubbed the palms of his hands on his jeans as he sat down. "I'm not altogether sure why Lily wanted me to see you. I assume it has to do with giving me information about her disease."

The doctor nodded. "Yes, that's definitely part of it. The other part is that I have personal experience with MS."

"She mentioned that." Nate sat back in the chair.

"My wife has MS. Her condition is fairly advanced. After talking with Lily, I thought maybe I could give you a perspective that she couldn't." The man cleared his throat.

"For the record, I was opposed to Lily's decision to end the engagement and leave town, but she was determined."

"Have you known Lily long?"

"From the day she was dropped off at the manor by her mother. My dad was originally the family doctor for the Collingworths. I took over when he retired twenty years ago."

That explained why he'd taken the interest he had in Lily. "You diagnosed her?"

Dr. Bennett nodded. "When she came in after the initial symptoms she'd suffered, I suspected, but she resisted testing at that point. Two months later she was back again with the same symptoms, along with a couple new ones. This time I insisted she get testing. She agreed only when I promised not to tell anyone of her condition. Of course, I wouldn't have anyway. Given patient confidentiality, I couldn't even if I had wanted to."

"How did I not know about what was going on with her?" Nate asked, as much to himself as the doctor.

"The symptoms she initially presented with were not major. In fact, had I not had the experience I did with my wife, I might not have come to the diagnosis as quickly." The doctor leaned forward, bracing his elbows on his thighs, his gaze direct. "I'm going to tell you right off the bat, life with MS can be easy and it can be difficult. My wife has gotten to the point where we don't have as many easy days anymore."

Nate frowned. "How old is your wife?"

"She's fifty-two. Up until about five years ago, she had long stretches where her MS didn't impact our life much at all. Unfortunately, for whatever reason, the progression of the disease has accelerated in the past few years. It has been a challenge to adjust. Even with my medical knowledge of the disease, it has still been a challenge."

"What has been the biggest adjustment?" Nate asked.

The man stared at him for a moment then said, "The change to the relationship both emotional and physical. Her frustration has increased as the disease has worsened. Emotionally she can be all over the map some days. Physically we are not as active anymore. We aren't able to participate in a lot of the things we used to as a couple and with our friends. Our intimate relationship also...changed."

Nate let the man's words sink in. He had never talked with his dad about how things had changed with his mom after she'd been diagnosed with cancer. She, too, had had good days and bad. But Nate had never really thought about how it would have affected their physical relationship. He'd been twenty when she'd first been diagnosed. Back then, he'd just preferred to think that his parents didn't have that type of relationship anymore. Stupid of him, but probably not uncommon for kids to assume when it came to their parents. Thinking about it now, he had to wonder how it would be to lose the ability to have that intimacy with someone you loved.

The doctor must have read the questions on his face because he said, "You adjust. It's not easy, but when you love the person, you adjust. And, really, the changes were more difficult on my wife than they were on me. On top of having to face the decline in her body and not being able to do the things she had enjoyed, she dealt with a lot of guilt that I was having to face those changes, too. Because of her. It made her very angry at times. Weepy at others."

"Has it continued to be that way?" Nate asked.

"Not to that extent. As time has passed, we've worked through the emotional side of things. And we just committed to finding new things we could do together. It's a choice, son. A choice to love. A choice to live."

Nate rubbed a hand over his face. Was he strong enough to be there for Lily the way she would need him to be in the future?

"Eli?"

Nate turned to see a woman in an electric wheelchair come into the room.

Dr. Bennett stood and went to her. "Hello, darling. You decided to join us."

"Yes. Something told me I should." The woman maneuvered the wheelchair closer to where Nate sat. She was a thin woman with shoulder-length graying hair that looked like it had once been a dark brown. Her eyes were a deep blue and looked at him with a mixture of curiosity and friendliness. Once in place, she lowered her hands to her lap. "I'm Beth Bennett."

Nate stood and held out his hand. "Nate Proctor."

After shaking it, she waved toward his chair. "I hear you want information about life with MS."

As Nate sat back down, he glanced at the doctor and then back to his wife. "Yes. Someone very special to me is dealing with it. She suggested I speak to the doctor."

The woman smiled. "Lucky you, you're going to get to speak to me, too."

When Nate left their home an hour later, he knew more about MS than he could ever have thought possible. Beth Bennett had held absolutely nothing back. She'd told him straight out the issues that Lily could face in the years ahead. It left him sick to his stomach to think of what she might have to endure.

And it seemed that one of the scariest parts of the disease was its unpredictability. It was possible that Lily could go for years without a major flare-up or worsening of the symptoms. But then again, it could happen tomorrow.

As he drove to his apartment, Nate thought back to what Beth had said as their conversation had wound down.

The best advice I can give is to live each day to its fullest. Don't worry about what may be coming. She'd tilted her head and smiled at him. *But then that's how we should live our lives regardless, right? No one is guaranteed tomorrow even if they are perfectly healthy.*

Nate realized that even though he'd had the experience

with his mom, he'd never truly embraced that philosophy. He'd been too worried trying to prepare things for the future. It was why he'd put off settling on a wedding date with Lily. He'd wanted things with the garages to be going well. He wanted to prove he was worthy of one of the Collingsworth sisters. Lily had so much money, but he had been determined to prove he could support her without it.

He didn't doubt that she had seen his reluctance to get married as a lack of commitment on his part. How could she trust his love when he hadn't even been willing to take that final step to marry her?

Nate pulled his car into the parking lot of the apartment block and sat staring blankly out the windshield. He no longer blamed her for running off to London the way she had. If she'd known everything back then that he knew now, it's no wonder she didn't think she could trust him to be there for her. Yeah, he had no one else to blame but himself for the lousy mess he ended up in.

He thumped his hand on the steering wheel before shoving the door of the truck open. After slamming it with more force than necessary, he strode toward the front door of the building and let himself in. His guts were churning with all the information he'd learned today and all the revelations about himself he'd had to face.

Right then, *he* was convinced that she really was better off without him. Though he loved her, he had never given her priority in his life the way he should have. With her sweet, understanding nature, she'd let him continually give priority to other things over the ones that were important to her. The things that should have been important to him, too. Like getting married.

As he walked into his apartment, the silence of it mocked him. If he hadn't screwed up so badly, he would be with Lily now. They would have faced her most recent flare-up together. He would have been the one to help her get cleaned up from her fall. He would have helped her get settled into bed and gotten her anything she needed. He would have slept beside her, able to wake at a moment's notice if she needed him. Instead, she was alone. And so was he.

ഗ‑ல

Though she really didn't want to, Lily knew she needed to spend a good portion of the next day in bed. Thankfully, when she woke Sunday morning, she was feeling significantly better. It was a relief that the symptoms had eased. Usually, that meant it was just a flare-up, not an exacerbation or worsening of the MS. She was going to have to take it easy for the next little while. Two flare-ups close together like that—even when she knew the reasons why— were scary and something to be avoided.

As she got ready for church, she chose a lightweight turquoise sundress with wide straps and a belt at the waist. It would give her a bit of a reprieve if it did turn out to be a warmer day than forecast. After applying a light layer of makeup, she brushed out the tangles in her hair and slipped on her shoes. All her movements were slow. Tentative. Testing. She still wasn't completely back to normal, but hopefully it would just take a little more time. She knew that each flare-up carried with it the possibility of more damage to her nerves and that this might be a new normal that she would have to adjust to.

Downstairs she found Amy and Lance preparing breakfast. As soon as Amy spotted her, she came and wrapped her arms around her.

"Thank you." Amy stepped back and looked right into her eyes. "Will told me all you did to help him with that dinner. And I know the price you paid. Thank you."

Lily smiled. "It was well worth it to help him give you such a romantic evening."

Amy lifted her left hand, diamond sparkling in the morning light. Though Will could have afforded a much bigger one, the dainty ring he'd had designed suited her perfectly. "I was so shocked. I honestly thought for sure I'd know when Will was planning to propose, but with your help he pulled off the perfect surprise."

Since Lily hadn't been around the previous day, the breakfast conversation surrounded the engagement and wedding plans. She tried not to experience a pang of jealousy when Amy mentioned that they hoped to get married soon. That, in fact, it was Will who was pressing for a short engagement rather than a long one. How she wished that had been the case with Nate. He had just never been interested in settling on a date. Soon. It had always just been soon.

And now it was just...never.

৩৩৩

Nate slid into the back pew of the church. Usually, he sat closer to the front, but he was late and grumpy and not really in the mood to be at church at all. The only reason he'd come, if he were totally honest, was to get a glimpse of Lily. He hoped that she was feeling well enough to come to the service today. He'd been thinking a lot about her since everything that had happened on Friday. Not that he hadn't been thinking about her to begin with, but it had been a lot more intense since finding out just exactly what she was dealing with and what the future might hold for her.

He looked down to the front of the sanctuary where the Collingsworth clan usually sat. His gaze skimmed the familiar figures and finally landed on Lily. She turned to talk to Amy, who was seated next to her. The smile that spread across her face kicked his heart into overdrive. As if she felt his gaze on her, she looked back in his direction.

Their gazes met and held. Her smile faded but then the corners of her mouth lifted into a quick smile before she turned back to face the front. Nate let out the breath he'd been holding. At least she hadn't ignored him. Had he smiled back? He wasn't sure...probably not. Smiling wasn't really his thing.

As the worship team began to sing, Nate tried to keep his focus on the service. He stood when those around him stood.

Sat when they sat and bowed his head when it was time to pray. When the pastor got up to preach, he was glad that the church was up to date with their technology so that any Scripture passages would appear on the screen at the front of the sanctuary. His Bible had gone up in flames along with everything else he'd owned and as yet, he hadn't replaced it. He supposed that spoke clearly as to his spiritual state of late.

"These past few weeks I've met with many people. They are Christians. They attend church, Bible studies, prayer meetings. They are wonderful people. And they're hurting. Oh, they're hurting." Pausing, the pastor rested his hand on his Bible. "Some question whether God really cares. Some wonder why they seem to have to deal with so much hurt when others don't. Some have just been so consumed by it all that they don't even try to figure it out—they're just trying to keep their heads above water."

That sounded familiar. Indeed, he did feel as if he'd just been trying to keep from going under ever since Lily had ended their engagement and walked away. Or maybe it had actually been before that. It probably went back as far as when his mother had begun to decline to the point where she could no longer function in the roles of wife and mother as she once had. And upon her death, his father had decided to bury his grief in work and started up the other garage in Sanford, which left more of the work at the one in Collingsworth to Nate. It was a burden he struggled under, particularly since he preferred to be under the hood of a car rather than behind a computer.

"Many use Job as an example of facing trials and still having a strong faith in God, but today I want to talk about a man who struggled, who sinned, who questioned God, who failed and yet, the Bible calls him a man after God's own heart. David." As he paused, a verse appeared on the screen. "Psalm 69. This whole psalm reveals the state of David's mind and heart as he faced many things in his life.

"Verse one says 'Save me, O God! For the waters have come up to my neck.' How many of us have felt this way? I'm sure if I asked for a show of hands, more than just a few would go up. He goes on to say 'I am weary with my crying; my throat is dry; my eyes fail while I wait for my God.' Have you felt that weariness? That overwhelming, soul deep, intense weariness? I have. David did. You are not alone."

Nate stared at the verses on the screen. He did feel alone. Very alone. With both his parents gone and no siblings, he'd felt that aloneness so strongly over the past couple of years. It was a strange disconnect between himself in the world. Like he had nowhere to plug himself in. And he had hated it. Hated that God had taken that connection away from him. First his mom. Then Lily and then his dad. It was like God had just set him adrift. Even when he'd been with Crystal there had been no connection there—she had seen it even when he hadn't.

"David knew he had sinned and failed God, but he—with a truly repentant heart—clung to the knowledge that God would rescue him. In Psalm 130, it says 'If You, Lord, should mark iniquities, Oh Lord, who could stand? But there is forgiveness with You, that You may be feared.' David knew that God would forgive him. And he knew that God would give him the strength to go through what he faced. There are times he pleads with God to take away his suffering, but at other times he praises God for the strength He gives him so that he could go through those trials."

The pastor's voice faded away as Nate bent his head and stared at his hands and at that moment let the weariness he'd been trying to hide—to hold back—wash over him. It swamped him completely, almost knocking him to his knees.

I can't do this anymore. I just can't.

With the weariness came emotion that he wouldn't allow to break through. His hands trembled as he struggled to draw breath into the tightness of his chest.

Help me, God.

"He is there for you. Make things right with Him. If you've sinned against Him. If you've walked away from Him.

If the things you've faced have pulled you away from His will, turn back now. God knows your heart. He knows your struggle. He wants to give you the strength—His strength—to face all those things. In Matthew 11 He says 'Come to Me, all you who labor and are heavy laden, and I will give you rest. Take My yoke upon you and learn from Me, for I am gentle and lowly in heart, and you will find rest for your souls.' If you're longing for that rest for your soul, turn to the Lord."

As the pastor finished his sermon, Nate felt that longing—so intense—to find rest for his soul. To let go of the burdens that had weighed him down for so long. He'd thought he could do it himself, but he knew now that no matter what he did on his own, he'd never truly find that rest and peace without the Lord. And though his mother had her ups and downs, she had believed that to her dying day.

As the opening strains of a hymn played on the piano, Nate felt his heart clench. It was a song he knew all too well. His mom had sung it so often, and in the last days of her life, she'd asked him to sing it for her. And he had, every time she asked. Though his voice had wavered with emotion, he had sung it for her.

When peace, like a river, attendeth my way,
When sorrows like sea billows roll;
Whatever my lot, Thou has taught me to say,
It is well, it is well, with my soul.

When the pastor asked for people to come to the front if they needed prayer, Nate stood and made his way on shaky legs out of the sanctuary into the foyer. He had to get out before emotion totally overtook him. Head bent, he walked to the door and leaned against it, trying to find the strength to push it open.

"Son?"

Son? He was no one's son anymore.

✑ Chapter Eighteen ✑

NATE froze, unwilling to look and see the man offering to pray with him. He couldn't let him see the emotion that was no doubt plastered all over his face. The man's hand covered his where it rested on the door and added his strength to push it open. Warmth greeted them as they stepped from the building.

Without a word, the man led Nate to the stone bench off to the side. The one he remembered seeing Lily sitting on that night not so long ago. The man's hand again moved to his shoulder as Nate sat, head bent, hands hanging loose between his knees as he leaned forward.

"Father, You know the burdens that Nate carries. He's faced so much over the past several years, no doubt he's felt overwhelmed and like he was going to drown. Today we ask that You give him rest from those burdens. Give him the strength to place them at Your feet and find the rest You want each of us to have. Assure him of Your love and Your grace for all he has faced and all he has done. Give him Your peace."

Nate felt tears spill over and lifted a hand to brush them

aside. He wasn't given to emotion, especially not tears. He drew in a ragged breath as the man finished his prayer. Finally, he looked over to see who it was that had seen his pain and offered to pray with him. Though he didn't know the man well, he recognized him right away as Megan's father.

The older man smiled at him. "You're not alone, son. I know you probably feel that you are, but know that there are people who cared about your parents and who care about you."

Nate gave a nod, wishing everything felt better, that he was flooded with the peace the man had prayed for him.

But he wasn't.

"Thank you. I appreciate the prayer."

"Anytime." The man held out his hand which Nate shook before he stood.

"I need to go."

The man nodded and stepped to the side so Nate could move past him. He laid a hand on his arm as he walked by. "I realize we haven't made much effort to connect with you after your dad died." The man frowned. "I let the busyness of life get the better of me, but I would like to make myself available to you if you ever need to talk. Megan has shared about what you've been dealing with most recently with Lily. Between that and the fire I'm sure you're feeling a bit overwhelmed. I'm a listening ear if you need one. No pressure. Just know the offer stands should you ever want to talk."

"Thank you," Nate said again, feeling a slow connection being made. He looked into the man's blue eyes and saw concern there, but also a serious intent. "I might just take you up on that."

"In the meantime, we will be praying for you."

After Nate had slid behind the wheel of his truck, he sat for a moment, pondering the tumult of thoughts and feelings that were so vibrantly alive within his mind and body. After his mother's death, he'd closed them off. Intense emotions could cause the most hurt in the end. He realized now that he'd held back so much from Lily even though he'd loved her with all his heart. He'd been scared to show exactly how much she'd meant to him. How important she was to him. And in the end, it had felt like it had been the right decision when she'd left him. And yet, would she have left him if he'd shown all along just how much she meant to him? He would never know now.

Movement from the corner of his eye caught his attention, and he saw people were beginning to leave the church. Needing to get away, Nate quickly put the truck in reverse and made his way out of the parking lot.

Nate pulled to a stop on the driveway and stared at the manor. He knew this was where he needed to come, but his stomach was a mass of nerves. After leaving the church that morning he'd gone to his apartment, but its stark emptiness had pulled him more to depression than the peace he sought. Instead, he'd gone to Walmart and picked up some fishing equipment and a fishing license. All of his fishing equipment—and his dad's—had been lost in the fire. After paying for it all, he made his way to the fishing spot he and his dad used to go to years ago. Before his mother had gotten sick and then died. Before his dad had decided to open the garage in Sanford. Back when their lives had been perfect.

And as he'd sat there, he had allowed himself to feel everything he'd been holding back for so long. Mainly it was the grief. Grief over the losses that had ripped at his heart. His mom. Lily. His dad. Each one had crushed him more than he had allowed himself to acknowledge. Alone at the water's edge, Nate hadn't caught any fish, but he'd shed the tears he'd never allowed to come before. And he'd made his way back to the Lord.

And as he did, he'd known that he needed to make things right. First with Crystal for how he'd been during their relationship. He should never have allowed their relationship to continue knowing he could never offer her his whole heart. It was wrong to have taken advantage of what she'd offered knowing that.

And now he was here to apologize to Lily.

He climbed from the truck and rounded the hood to head for the front door. As he waited for someone to answer his knock, he prayed he could do this. Right then it was just to ask for forgiveness. That was step one. The other steps would come in time...hopefully.

"Nate!" Will smiled at him. "C'mon in."

"Thanks," Nate said as he stepped past him into the foyer. "Is Lily here?"

"Yes, she is. I think she's on the back porch."

Nate hesitated then asked, "Is it okay if I go talk to her?"

Will stared at him for a second. "Are you planning to upset her?"

"I hope not. That's not my intention."

Will clapped him on the shoulder. "Then go for it."

Nate walked through the kitchen, out the back door. His gaze immediately found Lily. She sat in the swing at the far end of the porch, her head bent over a small bundle in her arms. The sight was like a kick in the gut.

Lily with a baby. If things had been different—

Nate cut the thought off. That was not why he was here. Today he was there to ask forgiveness from her. He couldn't allow himself to think beyond that just yet. He ran a hand through his hair as he slowly walked toward her.

"Lily?" He wished he'd worn a hat that he could have pulled off so he had something to do with his hands. Instead, he shoved them into his pockets and watched as she looked up, surprise spreading across her face.

"Nate? What are you doing here?"

He motioned to the chair placed not too far from the swing. "Can I talk to you for a minute?"

Her eyes widened as she nodded. "Have you met Daniel Joshua?" She leaned forward, moving the blanket from the baby's face. "Isn't he beautiful?"

Nate found himself nodding, even though he was pretty sure the little guy would have objected to being called beautiful if he could have voiced his thoughts. "How is he doing?"

"Really great. I offered to sit with him for a bit while Jessa and Lance took a walk down to the lake. Jess was cooped up for so long that she likes to be outside as much as possible. And I think she could use a little time with Lance, just the two of them."

Nate nodded, watching as she set the swing in motion with her foot. He didn't say anything at first, but then she looked up at him, curiosity on her face. He sat back in the chair and cleared his throat.

Rubbing at the leg of his jeans, he tried to pull his thoughts together. He'd rehearsed this several times before coming, but he hadn't counted on seeing Lily looking so beautiful with a baby in her arms. It had completely knocked him off track. "Ummm...I've come to apologize."

Lily's brow furrowed. "Apologize? For what?"

Nate stared out over the back yard for a moment before turning his gaze back to her. "I didn't treat you very well when we were together."

"What?" Lily tilted her head.

Nate looked down at the wooden boards beneath his feet. "I never gave you the priority I should have. I kept putting things off that I knew were important to you." He took a deep breath. "You deserved better than that. I knew that then and still chose to act the way I did."

"Why are you telling me this now?" Lily asked softly.

Because I love you with all my heart.

The words wrapped around Nate's chest like a vise, robbing him of breath for a second. "I need to make things right. Because I need peace."

She stared at him, her gaze intent and then she said, "The sermon this morning?"

"Yes. Since my mom's..." Nate paused and swallowed hard. "Since my mom's death, I've just been trying to keep my head above water. The fire was just kind of the last straw." Actually, finding out about her MS diagnosis was, but right now was not the time to bring that up. "I want to thrive, not just survive from day to day. And I realized today that no matter how well my business does, as long as I feel like I'm drowning under the other things that have happened to me, I will always just be in survival mode. I don't want that anymore."

Lily nodded. "I got to that point when I was dealing with my MS diagnosis as well. I needed to learn to accept it and be grateful for each day I was given instead of being dragged down into a depression over why it had to be me dealing with it. Can't say it was easy, but in the end it was worth it." She gave him a small smile. "Not saying I don't have down days— I do—but they aren't as frequent or as difficult as they once were."

"Yes, I figure I still have a ways to go with this, but this was where I needed to start."

"I understood more than you thought why you treated me the way you did. I made my peace with it and forgave you."

"But you still left. You didn't trust me."

Her eyes widened and then narrowed. "Yes, I suppose that's true. To some extent. But I know now that I also left out of fear. It wasn't as simple as just one thing. And in the end, it really was for the best. I needed to go through what I did in order to get to where I am now."

Nate nodded, though it was hard to hear her basically admit that breaking up with him had been for the best. It was the one reason he wasn't here to try to change her mind. He had to be willing to find peace in his life without her before attempting to see if she would give him a second chance. Why would she want to give their relationship another shot if he still needed to get himself together?

"Anyway, I won't take up any more of your afternoon. I just wanted to try and make this right with you. Thank you for giving me that opportunity."

"Nate—"

Whatever she'd been about to say got lost in the shrieks of two young girls as they burst through the back door and headed for the play structure. Will followed behind them, yelling their names. When they didn't respond, he turned to where Nate and Lily sat.

"Sorry, guys," he said, a rueful look on his face. "Amy didn't realize you were out here when she told the girls they could come out."

Nate stood. "That's okay. I was just leaving." He turned back toward the woman who held his heart. "Thanks again, Lily."

She nodded but didn't say anything.

He stuck out his hand toward Will. The other man took it in a firm shake. "See you around."

And even though the ache in his heart grew with each step he took away from Lily, Nate knew that it was what he had to do. Just as she felt she'd had to walk away from him, it was now his turn to walk away from her.

For now.

"Lily?"

Her gaze followed Nate as he walked away from her. Without a backward glance, he went down the back steps and around the corner of the manor. It felt as if her heart was being squeezed by a big hand—tighter and tighter—until she thought it would burst. In their seven years together, they'd never had such an emotional conversation. He had never talked about his feelings. He'd never talked about how things were between them. And he'd certainly never broached his own spiritual life. It was all she would have wanted...three years ago. If he'd been as honest with her then as he had been just now, she might not have left.

But now he was the one walking away from her. Was that it? He was making things right, asking forgiveness, in order to move forward in his life. Did any part of that have room for her? Or had she burned that bridge three years ago?

"Lily? Are you okay?"

The urgency in Will's voice drew her attention back to him. She stared at her brother as she tried to gather herself back together. "I'm fine."

He sat down in the chair so recently vacated by Nate. "He said he wouldn't upset you."

Was she upset? Yes, among other things, she was probably upset. But she was also stunned. "It's okay. It was a conversation we needed to have."

"Are you guys back..." Will's voice trailed off as she shook her head.

"It wasn't about that. This was about our past. About the way he'd treated me."

Will's brow furrowed as his expression darkened. "Did he hurt you? You never said anything about that."

Again Lily shook her head. "No, it wasn't like that." Her gaze dropped to the sleeping baby in her lap. Did she want to share the pain she'd felt back then? The pain that had led to her decision to leave Collingsworth three years ago? She stroked a finger down the baby's soft cheek. "Back then, Nate worked our relationship into the available spaces in his life. I know it seemed like we spent a lot of time together, but it was only as long as his mom and dad or the garage hadn't already taken that time. There were many times I asked if we could go someplace or do something when he'd say no because the garage needed him or his mom or dad did. I kind of felt like I'd been penciled in at the bottom of his priority list."

"I didn't know," Will said, leaning forward to rest his elbows on his thighs.

"You were caught up in other things." Lily looked out across the back yard in the direction Jessa and Lance had gone. "Everyone was. Even though I wasn't his first priority, my relationship with Nate gave me some feeling of having a place in someone's life."

She glanced at Will as he let out a long sigh. "I'm sorry, Lil. You did kind of get lost in the shuffle back then, didn't you?"

"It shouldn't have mattered, but I needed to grow up a bit to understand that. These past three years have helped me to do that."

"Are you going to give Nate a second chance?" Will asked.

Lily took a deep breath and let it out. "He didn't ask for one."

❦ Chapter Nineteen ❧

BY Thursday, Lily felt confident enough to take her car into town to run some errands. First up was an appointment with the doctor. After her latest flare-up, she just wanted to touch base with him to make sure he didn't feel she should have any testing done. As she pulled into the parking lot of the office, Lily said a prayer of thanks that her doctor was so in tune with MS and its many facets. He understood that peace of mind was important, particularly after flare-ups or attacks. He'd willingly made time for Lily when she'd called, and she knew he wouldn't rush her through their appointment by brushing off any concerns she had.

"Hi, Lily," Dr. Bennett said as he walked into the small room. He hitched his pants before sitting down at the desk. Without even looking at the file he said, "So I hear you had a flare-up."

She gave him the run down and then together they discussed what had caused it and the steps she'd taken afterward. He didn't think there was a need for another scan since she'd had one not too long ago, but was willing to set one up if she pressed.

"I think I'll pass this time, but if I have another flare-up within the next month, maybe we should consider it."

The doctor nodded his agreement then sat back in his chair. "So...I enjoyed meeting your young man. He had plenty of questions."

Lily stared at him, a pit growing in her stomach. Nate had talked to him? Why hadn't he said something? "He didn't mention that to me."

One of the doctor's eyebrows arched. "Really? He was at our house for almost two hours. Talked to both me and Beth."

And got enough information to scare him off for good, apparently. "Thank you so much for taking the time to speak with him. I wasn't sure he was going to take advantage of your offer."

"Yeah, I felt for him. I remember being in his shoes—facing that unknown—and I was even a doctor. It's completely different when the diagnosis hits someone you love."

Lily nodded. But apparently in the end, Nate had taken the information he'd been given and breathed a big ol' sigh of relief. Pain lanced through her heart. She still wasn't worthy of his time. He'd heard how much time would have to be devoted to her because of the MS and had been grateful that he'd dodged that bullet.

As she left the doctor's office and headed to her next errand, Lily gave herself a lecture. She had no right to be upset by all of this. After all, she had been the one to end things with Nate. She had kept her secret and run for Europe. That alone gave her no right to be upset that Nate had decided to accept what she'd done three years ago and move on after making peace with his past.

It was a thought she needed to keep front and center as she pushed open the door of the bridal salon.

❧◌❧

Nate stepped out of the small hardware store, coming to a stop when he recognized Lily's vehicle pulling into the strip mall parking lot. He waited to see if she spotted him, but she kept her head bent as she climbed out and, surprisingly, headed for the bridal salon. He stood there for a moment trying to figure out what she was doing there. Maybe it had to do with Amy and Will's upcoming nuptials since they were engaged now.

Before he could stop himself, Nate headed toward where her car was parked. His steps faltered when she came out of the store more quickly than he had anticipated. She held a long white dress bag and walked to her car without looking around.

"Hey, Lily," Nate said as he came up behind her.

She spun around, folding the dress bag over her arm and pulling it close. "Nate? I didn't see you."

"I was just in at Joe's." He nodded his head toward the hardware store. With a glance at the dress bag, he asked, "Getting ready for Amy and Will's wedding already?"

She stared at him for a moment before shaking her head. "No. This is *my* wedding dress."

It couldn't have taken him more off-guard or hurt more if a horse had kicked him in the gut. *Her wedding dress?* They hadn't even settled on a date, but she had a dress?

Nate shoved his hands into his pockets. "I didn't know you had bought one."

Lily shrugged. "I found it one day when I came into the shop to try on dresses."

"You didn't mention going dress shopping with anyone."

"I didn't. I went by myself. I hadn't planned to buy anything, but as soon as I put it on, I knew."

Though her words were steady, the soft tone pulled at his heart. She'd gone dress shopping by herself. Found her dream dress by herself and hadn't even told him. No doubt because he hadn't been willing to set a date.

"I don't understand. Why are you picking it up now?"

"They have been storing it for me for the past three years." Her chin lifted slightly. "I picked it up today because I'm probably going to be selling it."

Selling it? The one-two punch pushed the air from his lungs. Words failed him at that point. He wanted to tell her not to do that, but if she wasn't interested in a relationship with him, then it made sense that she would want to sell it. Given who she was, she didn't have to do it for the money, so it must mean that it was one more lose end she wanted to tie up.

He took a deep breath as she turned from him and opened the back door of her car. She leaned in and laid the bag across the back seat. When she shut the door, she gave him a small smile. "Gotta keep going. Have a few errands I need to finish up today."

Nate nodded and stepped up onto the sidewalk in front of the strip mall. "See you around."

As her car backed out of the spot, he turned and walked to where his truck was parked. Well, now what did he do? He had hoped he'd have some time to get a handle on exactly where she was emotionally. If she might be willing to reconsider a relationship with him. Some of the vibes she was sending out could easily be taken either way, but her dismissal of him the other night at the manor was a hard one to take. And now she was going to sell her wedding dress? The one she'd bought to marry him in?

Nate knew he had to step things up and give it one final push. If she said no, he would accept that and move on as best he could. But maybe...just maybe...she could see that he'd changed and would give him a second chance.

ଙ୨∞ଔ

Lily laid the bag out on the bed. It had been three years since she'd last seen it. Would she still love it as much now as she had that day she'd tried it on? With slow movements she unzipped the bag and pushed the sides to open it. She ran her fingers over the tulle that made up the skirt of the soft blush-colored gown. No one had ever seen the dress except her and the women in the bridal shop.

Her family had already been asking about the wedding date once they were engaged. Lily had been afraid that they'd think her foolish for buying a dress without a firm date. She really hadn't planned to buy one when she'd gone in that day to try on dresses. But it had been just perfect. All the women in the shop had agreed. And it wasn't like she hadn't had the money. So she'd ended up with a wedding dress and no wedding.

She'd told Nate she was going to sell it, but as she looked at it there on her bed, she just couldn't imagine letting it go to another bride. Reaching in, she pulled the hanger out and carefully freed the dress from the bag. Her breath caught as she once again saw it in all its beauty. It was all she'd remembered and more. Part of her wanted to try it on, but she knew that there was no way she could do it on her own. Instead she hung it up on a hook on the door leading to the bathroom then sat back down on the bed and stared at it.

She couldn't believe she'd run into Nate right at that moment. He'd looked shocked when she'd told him what it was and what she intended to do with it. Did he still have the ring he'd given her? Or had that been burned in the fire along with the rest of his things?

A knock on her door sent her scrambling off the bed. She was relieved to see Julia standing in the doorway. "Mom said to tell you supper's ready."

"Thanks, sweetie. I'll be right down."

With one last glance at the dress, Lily headed down to join her family. Decisions about the dress could be made later. There was no rush.

❧❧

"Nate's here."

Lily looked up from her laptop at Amy's words. She'd been working to get caught up on the blog she wrote as well as the emails she received as a result of it. After she'd come to accept what was happening to her, she had found writing blog posts had helped to channel her fears, frustrations and other emotions. As people discovered it, the blog had grown in popularity. Unfortunately, she'd neglected it since her move from London.

"Is he here to see me?" Lily asked as she set her laptop on the bed beside her and unfolded her legs.

"Yep. Asked if you were around."

"Okay. Just give me a second. I'll be right down."

Once Amy had left her, Lily stood and went to the bathroom to make sure she looked presentable. Curiosity had her moving a little more quickly than usual. It had been a couple of days since they'd met up on the sidewalk in front of the bridal shop. Could their encounter there have brought about this visit?

"He's in the library," Amy told her when she walked into the kitchen.

Spinning on her heel, Lily made her way to the library and found Nate standing at the bay window looking out across the driveway.

"Hi, Nate. Amy said you wanted to see me."

He swung around and for a moment, just stared at her. She drank in the sight of him, too. The light sprinkling of gray that had just started to show when she'd left was more pronounced now. Early gray had run in his family, but Lily knew it was likely due to stress as well. In her eyes it had just made him more handsome.

"Yes. Sorry to show up without calling." He pulled his hand from his pocket and gestured to the desk. "I was hoping you'd be willing to help me out again."

"Sure." Lily tried to quell the disappointment that welled

up within her. This was about business. "I did offer, right?"

Nate nodded. "But if you've changed your mind, I understand."

Lily watched as he pulled the laptop from the bag and opened it up. She moved to stand on the other side of the desk. When he glanced up at her, she said, "I heard you went to talk to Dr. Bennett."

One of his eyebrows lifted as he reached for the cable of the monitor that was still there from the last time she'd worked on his paperwork. "He called you?"

"No, I had an appointment with him yesterday. He mentioned that they had spoken with you."

Nate's movements stilled. "Is everything okay?"

"Yes. I just wanted to touch base with him after what happened on Friday." She paused. "I didn't think you were going to take him up on the offer to talk."

Nate shrugged and looked back down at the laptop. "To be honest, I wasn't sure what the purpose of having me talk to him was."

Lily clasped her hands together. She didn't know how to respond to that. The fact that it had taken so long for him to call Dr. Bennett left her wondering if she'd made a mistake in offering the opportunity to him. "Why did you go?"

He didn't answer right away. Lily wondered if he'd actually heard her since he kept his gaze on the laptop, even when he straightened and rested his hands on his hips. Finally, he looked up. She saw him swallow hard before he said, "Seeing you on the path Friday night was...difficult. I had to know more about what was happening to you."

Lily felt her heart clench at the flash of emotion on his face. "I'm sorry if I scared you. I didn't know you were at the manor when I called."

"You didn't just scare me. You scared Lance and your sisters, too." Nate looked back down at the laptop and then pulled some papers from the bag.

Feeling like she'd just been reprimanded, Lily frowned. It hadn't been the best decision she'd ever made to keep working in the heat, but she'd done it for a good cause. Couldn't Nate see that? If she hadn't been able to finish, Will wouldn't have been able to have the perfect moment he wanted for Amy.

Lily looked down at the top of the desk. Emotions warred within her, just one more thing she could thank the MS for. She had never been a hugely emotional person and it took a lot to make her cry, but right then she just wanted to go upstairs, throw herself across her bed and sob. She took a couple of deep breaths, willing the emotions to subside.

Focus on the job.

Hoping her voice would stay steady, she asked, "So is this just basically more of the same?"

Though she sensed Nate's gaze on her, Lily kept looking at the pile of paper next to the laptop. She didn't want to take the chance that he could read anything in her expression. When the silence stretched between them, Lily finally looked up.

"Yes, it's just more receipts and some payments and deposits to record." He paused. "Are you sure you're up for this? Feel free to tell me no."

Oh, she wanted to say no, but not because she wasn't up for the work. It was slowly dawning on her that she'd been lying to herself all along. When she'd come back and found out that Nate wasn't seeing anyone, she'd told herself it didn't matter, when in fact it had. She desperately wanted to be back with him, but now she had to face the lasting consequences of her decision three years ago. She'd ended things and it no longer mattered if she'd had a change of heart. Whatever he might have felt initially, he no longer seemed interested in picking up where they'd left off.

"It's fine. I should be done with it in a couple of hours." Lily waited for him to move from behind the desk before going around it the opposite way to reach the chair. "If I have questions, I'll give you a call."

Nate nodded. "Thank you."

"You're welcome," Lily said as she picked up the first piece of paper off the pile. Only when she heard him move away did she raise her gaze and watch him walk out of the library. Her vision blurred as she looked down at the paper in her hand. A tear dropped on the paper. She swiped at the moisture on her cheeks. Resting the paper in her lap, she took several deep breaths before focusing on it again.

❧

Nate wanted to kick himself. There had been so many openings during that conversation, and he'd let each one pass. It was like the words had been stuck in his throat. All he could do was stare at her and wish she could read his mind. That she could feel what was in his heart. It would have been so much easier than trying to find the words to say without messing up completely.

As he sat behind the wheel of his truck, Nate stared straight ahead. He had come here with work as an excuse, but at every opening he froze. Why? He knew it was partly because if she said no, the last spark of hope would be gone. But...if she felt the same way, he was just wasting time. He was just a coward if he put it off any longer.

He'd been praying hard about it. Spending time in prayer and reading the Bible had been something he'd tried to give priority to over the past few days. Why couldn't he trust God with this? Why couldn't he believe that God would give him the strength to continue on even if Lily said no?

He thumped the steering wheel with his fists. Now or never. He couldn't continue on in this limbo.

Please, God, let her be willing to hear me out.

Determined not to allow fear to overcome him, Nate strode toward the manor. He walked in without knocking this time and headed straight for the library. When he entered the room, Lily's head lifted and she stared at him, her eyes wide and suspiciously damp.

Love, determination and hope propelled him to where she sat.

He braced his hands on the desk and leaned toward her. "Here's the thing. I'm scared. You didn't trust me three years ago when you found out about your MS. And now I understand why you felt that way. And I even think you did the right thing. But now...now I'm asking you for another chance." If possible, Lily's eyes widened even further. "I know what the future might hold for you. I understand the demands MS might—will—place on you and on our relationship. But none of it matters. All I want is a chance to show you that you can depend on me. That I will be there for you regardless of how things are in the years ahead. I just..."

Nate winced as his voice cracked. He swallowed hard and continued, "I just love you so much. Give me a chance to prove that to you the proper way this time around."

His heart clenched when he saw tears well up in Lily's eyes. Like him, she wasn't one given to crying, so the sight pulled the breath from his lungs. "I didn't mean to make you cry. If you don't feel the same way, I understand. I just want you to know that the MS doesn't make any difference in how I feel about you. With or without it, I would want to be with you...if you'll have me."

When she didn't reply, but just sat there staring at him, Nate straightened. He tried to push aside the dread he felt, bracing himself for what was to come. It was a risk he had to take, and there was no going back. He'd laid it all out there. Now it was up to her.

Slowly she stood and as she moved to walk around the desk, Nate wasn't sure if she was going to walk out on him or if he should meet her half way. But when he realized she wasn't heading for the door, he took two steps toward her then stopped. "Lily?"

"Oh, Nate." Lily threw herself at him, her arms going tight

around his shoulders.

As he pulled her close into his embrace, Nate buried his face in her hair, breathing in the familiar scent. She pulled back enough to press her lips to his. "I love you, too, Nate. I never stopped."

The final barrier he'd kept in place broke down and the love he felt for this woman rushed over him. The fear that had held him back all those years was gone. He knew without any doubt that he could—and would—give Lily the priority she deserved in his life. God first. Then Lily. Then everyone else. She would never again wonder if she could trust his love. With God's help, he would make sure of that.

❧ *Epilogue* ☙

LILY stared into the mirror as the makeup artist worked on her face and someone else worked on her hair. She was glad to not have to do all this herself, but bittersweet emotions still filled her.

Amy and Will were getting married. Just four short months after their engagement they were getting married. There was snow on the ground and Christmas was just around the corner, but the focus of the Collingsworth family had been the wedding.

Lily had been glad for the distraction. It had kept her from wondering why her left hand was still bare. She touched her ring finger as the makeup artist asked her to close her eyes. For some reason she'd assumed that as soon as they were back together again Nate would pop the question. Instead, though their relationship was strong and growing stronger, there had been no talk of an engagement, let alone a marriage.

Thankfully she hadn't had any major attacks over the past few months. She'd made sure to find that balance in her life. She worked at Nate's garage doing the admin side of things for a couple of hours each day and had also become active in the MS support group in Collingsworth. Life was no longer clouded by what lay ahead for her in terms of her health. She and Nate had agreed to take it a day at a time.

With things going so well, it just made her all the more eager to begin their life together. Instead it felt like a repeat of what had happened four years ago when he had been reluctant to set a date. At this point she'd be happy with a wedding in Vegas. She just wanted to be Nate's wife.

"You look beautiful!"

Even with her eyes closed, Lily recognized Jessa's voice and smiled

"How's Amy doing?" Lily asked. "She nervous?"

"Not sure nervous is the word. She's pretty much over the moon excited."

"You can open now," the makeup artist told her.

Lily looked in the mirror again, a bit surprised at how much time they were taking with her. "You've done a wonderful job."

"It's easy when you give us so much to work with. Your cheekbones are to die for."

Lily smiled at her. "Thank you."

"Just a little bit more and you're done."

Sure enough, a short time later there was a cloud of hair spray and then they pronounced her perfect. Lily felt anything but perfect, but at least she knew she looked good.

"Where is everyone else?" Lily asked Jessa when the makeup and hair people left.

"They've gone to the bride's room at the chapel to get dressed. As soon as you're done here, you can go there, too."

Amy had chosen to have her best friend from Dallas, Lily and Cami as her bridesmaids. The other two had had their hair and makeup done first. Lily thought they should have just had their hair and makeup done at the chapel instead of the manor since that's where they were getting dressed, but since it was Amy's wedding, she was the one calling the shots.

There was a knock on the door of her room, and Jessa went to answer it. Alone, Lily sat staring at the mirror. Would Nate think she was beautiful? He told her often she was. He took care of her like he always had, and never let her doubt that he loved her.

So why didn't he just propose already?

"Lily?"

Shocked to hear his voice, Lily turned from her makeup table, gripping the front of the dressing gown she wore. Her eyes widened when she saw the man who had dominated her thoughts so much lately standing there. "Nate? What are you doing here?"

He looked so handsome in the black tuxedo he wore. As a groomsman for Will, he also wore a dark green bow tie that matched the dark green of the dresses the bridesmaids were to wear. Even though he'd once made her promise he wouldn't have to wear a tux at their wedding, he had been willing to wear one for Will's.

He smiled at her, and her heart skipped a beat.

"You look beautiful," he said as he moved to stand in front of her. "As always."

"I need to get dressed. You shouldn't be here."

"Here is *exactly* where I should be," Nate said. He brought his hand from behind his back as he lowered himself to one knee.

Lily's mouth went dry as she realized what was coming. Finally! "Yes!"

Nate lifted an eyebrow, amusement sparkling in his eyes. "You're supposed to let me ask you the question first."

She reached out to cup his face in her hands and looked into his eyes. "Okay. Ask me."

"Lily-belle, I love you so much. I can't imagine living my life without you. Will you do me the honor of becoming my wife?"

There was so much emotion in his eyes that Lily's breath caught. Oh yes, this man loved her as much as she loved him. "Yes. Oh, yes."

Nate reached for her left hand and held it in his own. "This is not the same one I proposed with last time. That one got burned in the fire, but I hope you love this one just as much."

She looked at it, trying desperately to keep the tears from flowing over and ruining her makeup. "It's beautiful. I love it because you gave it to me. It's perfect." Then she looked up at him and pinned him with a determined look. "But I'm not waiting very long for you to set the wedding date this time. I want to take a page out of Will and Amy's book and get married sooner rather than later."

Nate stood and drew her to her feet as well. He leaned forward and pressed a kiss to her lips. "How about we take a page out of Will and Amy's book and get married today?"

Lily stared at him, shock coursing through her. "Today?"

"Knowing that stress often aggravates your MS, Amy suggested that we have a double wedding, but not put any pressure on you to plan it." Nate held her hands tightly in his. "Are you okay with that? If not, that's fine. It will just be Will and Amy's wedding, and we can do ours on a different day."

Lily shook her head. "No. Today is perfect."

"Then let's go to the chapel so you can get dressed." Nate turned toward the door and called out, "Jessa?"

Jessa came back into the room, a wide smile on her face. "Congratulations!"

"You knew about this?"

"Of course! We've been busily planning it. We even snuck your dress over to the chapel while you were taking a shower earlier." Jessa pressed a kiss to her cheek. "Ready to go?"

Violet, Laurel and Cami were waiting for her in the foyer of the chapel. After hugging her, Laurel said, "Let's get you into the room and into your dress. The guests will be arriving soon.

Nate grabbed her hand and pulled her close. He kissed her softly before releasing her. "Meet me at the altar, Lily-belle."

"I will."

Inside the bridal room, Lily immediately sought out Amy. Her soon-to-be sister-in-law wore a white gown with a lace overlay that skimmed her curves and then flared out at mid-thigh. Her blonde curls hung long and loose under the headpiece and veil she wore. She was positively beaming.

"I can't even begin to thank you for this."

Amy's smile widened. "Are you sure you're okay sharing your wedding with me?"

"That's the question I should be asking *you*," Lily said. "I'm still in shock."

"I wanted this. After the rough roads we both traveled to get to this point, I think it's only fitting we share this final step."

"You need to get dressed," Cami said. "Unless you want to walk down the aisle dressed like that."

"Never!" Lily gave Amy a quick hug. "Thank you, again."

Heart pounding, Lily allowed her sisters to help her into the dress that was still as perfect as it had been three years earlier. "How is this even possible? We didn't apply for a wedding license or anything."

"Don't worry about that," Jessa said. "Today you will be married before God, and next week Nate said you guys will make it legal."

As Cami drew the zipper up her back, Lily asked, "Will we have to wait until then to...you know?"

Everyone in the room burst out laughing.

"I would imagine that's up to you and Nate," Cami said. "But in the eyes of God, you will be married today."

Married! Lily could hardly believe it. This had been planned perfectly for her. All the joy but none of the stress that might have debilitated her or prevented her from enjoying her wedding day.

"Are you happy?" Nate asked as he came up behind her. He ran his hands down her arms.

"Yes. So very happy." Lily turned from the large glass window and slid her hands behind his neck, interlacing her fingers. She went up on her tiptoes and pressed her lips to his in a lingering kiss. "I can't believe how you planned all of this. That you knew to get this place for us."

"It took some doing, but your sisters were more than willing to help me out."

After their church wedding, Nate had whisked her off to Vegas for a legal ceremony and then after one night there, they'd caught another flight bound for Switzerland and the chalet she'd rented during her time in London. Lily was positive she was going to wake up and find it was all a dream. It was all just that perfect.

"Just tell me you're not upset with me for waiting to propose and then making you share your wedding day."

Lily leaned against him, relishing the feel of him in her arms. The steady beat of his heart beneath her ear. "I'm so very much *not* upset. I couldn't have asked for anything more perfect. If I'd had to plan a wedding, I probably would have had to sleep for a week afterward."

A corner of Nate's mouth lifted. "Well, that wouldn't have been any fun, now would it?"

Warmth spread up Lily's cheeks. "No, no fun at all."

Before she realized his intent, Nate had slipped an arm under her knees and swung her up. He laid her on the big rustic bed she'd spent so many nights alone in and settled down next to her. "We've got two whole weeks here. Think that's enough time?"

"It's plenty. And when it's over, I will be more than ready to go home and start our new life together." She slid her hands into his hair and pulled him down for another kiss, deeper, longer, sweeter this time. "I love you, Nate."

"I love you too, baby. For now and forever."

❧ The End ❧

OTHER TITLES AVAILABLE BY

Kimberly Rae Jordan
(Christian Romances)

Marrying Kate

Faith, Hope & Love

Waiting for Rachel (*Those Karlsson Boys: 1*)
Worth the Wait (*Those Karlsson Boys: 2*)
The Waiting Heart (*Those Karlsson Boys: 3*)

Home Is Where the Heart Is (*Home to Collingsworth: 1*)
Home Away From Home (*Home to Collingsworth: 2*)
Love Makes a House a Home (*Home to Collingsworth: 3*)
The Long Road Home (*Home to Collingsworth: 4*)
Her Heart, His Home (*Home to Collingsworth: 5*)
Coming Home (*Home to Collingsworth: 6*)

A Little Bit of Love:
A Collection of Christian Romance Short Stories

**For more details on the availability of these titles,
please go to**

www.KimberlyRaeJordan.com

Contact

Please visit Kimberly Rae Jordan on the web!
Website: www.kimberlyraejordan.com
Facebook: www.facebook.com/AuthorKimberlyRaeJordan
Twitter: twitter.com/Kimberly Jordan

16980899R00129

Printed in Great Britain
by Amazon